SPECIAL MESSAGE TO READERS

This book is published under the auspices of

THE ULVERSCROFT FOUNDATION

(registered charity No. 264873 UK)

Established in 1972 to provide funds for research, diagnosis and treatment of eye diseases. Examples of contributions made are: —

A Children's Assessment Unit at Moorfield's Hospital, London.

•

Twin operating theatres at the Western Ophthalmic Hospital, London.

•

A Chair of Ophthalmology at the Royal Australian College of Ophthalmologists.

•

The Ulverscroft Children's Eye Unit at the Great Ormond Street Hospital For Sick Children, London.

You can help further the work of the Foundation by making a donation or leaving a legacy. Every contribution, no matter how small, is received with gratitude. Please write for details to:

THE ULVERSCROFT FOUNDATION,
The Green, Bradgate Road, Anstey,
Leicester LE7 7FU, England.
Telephone: (0116) 236 4325

In Australia write to:

THE ULVERSCROFT FOUNDATION,
c/o The Royal Australian College of Ophthalmologists,
27, Commonwealth Street, Sydney,
N.S.W. 2010.

Books by Corba Sunman
in the Linford Western Library:

RANGE WOLVES
LONE HAND
GUN TALK

TRIGGER LAW

Chuck Manning was working as a Texas Ranger when his Uncle Mort died in Clearwater County, leaving Chuck the Double M cattle ranch. But he learned that his Uncle had been murdered and small ranchers were being frightened into selling out. The county was plagued by night-riders, who rustled stock and killed without compunction. With nothing more than the reputation of the Rangers to back him, plus his own remarkable skills, Chuck set about righting the wrongs.

CORBA SUNMAN

TRIGGER LAW

Complete and Unabridged

LINFORD
Leicester

First published in Great Britain in 1998 by
Robert Hale Limited
London

First Linford Edition
published 2001
by arrangement with
Robert Hale Limited
London

British Library CIP Data

Sunman, Corba
Trigger law.—Large print ed.—
Linford western library
1. Western stories
2. Large type books
I. Title
823.9′14 [F]

ISBN 0–7089–9753–8

Published by
F. A. Thorpe (Publishing)
Anstey, Leicestershire

Set by Words & Graphics Ltd.
Anstey, Leicestershire
Printed and bound in Great Britain by
T. J. International Ltd., Padstow, Cornwall

This book is printed on acid-free paper

1

Chuck Manning spotted the drab buildings of Oaktown rising up in the distance of the illimitable Texas range and reined in his weary buckskin. Twisting in the saddle, he studied his back trail, his brown eyes narrowing under the wide brim of his tall-crowned black Stetson as he looked for movement in the searing heat haze clinging to the parched, short-grass range.

Seeing no movement behind, he pushed back his Stetson and wiped his bronzed forehead on the sleeve of his dusty red shirt. For a moment he relaxed, slipping his right foot out of the stirrup and crooking the leg around the saddlehorn while he reached into his shirt pocket and extracted a pack of Durham and brown cigarette papers. He continued to watch his back trail while rolling a smoke, then licked the thin paper and sealed it. He struck a match, lit the slim cylinder, then broke the match in two and dropped it to the grass.

A sigh escaped him as he drew on the cigarette, and some of the tension seeped out of his harsh features. He was a big man, two inches over six feet in height, with wide shoulders and a slim waist, his tough body honed to hardness by his grim way of life. His dark eyes were slitted against the glare of the sun that was almost too bright even beneath his down-pulled hatbrim, and tiny wrinkles formed crowsfeet in the taut skin surrounding them. Dressed in dusty range clothes, he wore a .45 Colt sixgun in a dark, scuffed holster tied down on his right thigh.

He instinctively checked his back trail again, then returned his foot to the stirrup and straightened his slumped shoulders. Riding forward, he kept his gaze on Oaktown, aware that his arrival there would multiply his problems. He had been down on the Mexican border on a gun chore when word reached him that his only kin, an uncle, Mort Manning, had recently died and left him the Double M ranch in Clearwater County, Texas.

Urging the buckskin into a faster gait, he was suddenly impatient to hit town and slake his thirst with a couple of beers. He had ridden a lonely trail for more than two weeks and, now he had reached the range where his inheritance awaited, he had to decide whether or not to pick up the threads of a new life in this desolate region south of the Red River and east of the New Mexico line or continue to ride with the Texas Rangers, policing this turbulent, primitive land of fierce passions and convulsive trigger fingers.

Oaktown sprawled its adobe buildings along the meandering trail that led north to the Red River. Manning reined in on the outskirts of the dusty community to look around and his tired buckskin snorted and jerked its head in the direction of the nearby livery barn.

Manning grinned and patted the animal's dusty neck.

'I guess you've earned a rest.' He reined towards the barn, dismounted, and led the horse to a drinking trough, where he stood looking around while the animal drank its fill. He was a tall, forbidding figure wearing shot-gun chaps, his drab range clothes streaked with trail dust. He stood flexing the powerful muscles in his legs, which were cramped by his long ride, and stretching his arms to get the kinks out of his powerful shoulders.

'Howdy, stranger.' A youthful voice greeted him from behind, and Manning glanced over a broad shoulder to look at the youth who emerged from the barn. 'Looks like you've ridden a fair piece.'

'Yeah. I have at that. Take care of the horse, huh? Give him the best.' He produced a silver dollar and flipped it into the youth's ready hand. 'I'll be stopping over several days.'

'Sure thing.' The youngster deftly

caught the coin.

Manning slid his Winchester out of the saddle boot and slung his saddle-bags across his left shoulder. He patted the buckskin's rump and kicked through the dust to the street. Evening was almost upon the range and silence lay heavily over the sleepy-looking town. There were only three horses visible along the whole length of the wide, rutted street, and they were standing together at a hitching rail in front of a saloon.

Manning walked to the saloon and shouldered through the batwing doors. He paused on the threshold to look around. Four men were playing cards at one of the six small tables on the left and there was a tall, heavily built tender wiping glasses behind the bar on the right. Manning hefted his rifle and walked to the bar, his spurs tinkling. He placed his saddle-bags on the polished surface of the bar and propped the Winchester against it.

'You serve food?' He moistened his

lips at the thought of filling his stomach.

'Sure thing. You particular what you eat?' The tender's narrowed eyes flickered over Manning's figure, probing, trying to gauge what lay beyond the dusty appearance.

'Anything you got to hand. I'm hungrier than a lobo wolf. Been on the trail a couple of weeks. Gimme a whisky and a beer.'

The tender nodded and served him. Manning flipped a dollar on to the polished surface of the bar, making it ring sharply in the silence. As the tender departed to the kitchen one of the card players arose from the table and came across to the bar, his spurs tinkling musically. A tall, powerful man, he paused a couple of feet to Manning's left, and Manning glanced at him over the rim of his beer glass as he drank thirstily.

The man was dressed in range clothes; green shirt, short leather vest and brush-scratched leather batwing chaps. His riding boots were dusty, and the long spurs fastened to them were equipped with vicious Spanish rowels. A black Stetson was pushed back off his forehead to reveal yellowish hair. His eyes were blue, filled with arrogance. His right hand was resting lightly on the black butt of the Colt sixgun snug in a tied-down holster, his fingers tapping impatiently on the bone grip.

Manning did not interrupt his drinking, and was aware that the men at the card table were intent on watching their companion.

'Where you from?' The man's voice was harsh, deep-toned, sounding as if it started from somewhere around his knees, and it contained an unmistakable sneer.

Manning set down his half-empty glass and wiped his mouth with the back of his left hand. Acting as if he hadn't heard the question, he drank the whisky at a gulp, then finished the beer.

'Whatsa matter with you?' demanded the man. 'Don't you hear so good? I asked you a question.'

'I heard.' Manning's voice rasped in the silence.

The man waited until it became obvious that Manning had nothing more to say then pushed back his shoulders. 'What's your business in town?' he demanded belligerently.

'My business in town is — my business.' Manning's tone was soft. He looked squarely at the man, whose expression slowly hardened at the raw challenge in Manning's voice.

'You're a stranger so I'll go easy on you, mister,' he said. 'I'm Keno Jackson.'

'Is that supposed to mean something to me?' Manning turned slightly to confront the man, his right hand down at his side. He could feel the butt of his holstered gun touching the inside of his wrist. Outwardly he appeared casual, but inside he was like a coiled spring waiting to flash into action.

'If it doesn't then you better step light. Mebbe you ain't the man I'm on the look-out for.'

'Who would that be?'

'Feller by the name of Manning.'

'What's he guilty of?' Manning gave no hint of recognizing his own name.

'All I wanta know is your handle,' snapped Jackson.

'It ain't Manning.' Manning half-turned back to the bar and Jackson reached out and grasped his left elbow, pulling him back face to face. Manning's reaction was lightning fast. His gun rasped out of its holster and the muzzle dug painfully into Jackson's hard midriff as he jerked back his right fist to throw a punch.

'Yuh better back off and butt out before this goes too far,' he advised. 'If yuh got something sticking in your craw then spit it out pronto.'

Jackson's heavy face changed expression. He looked down, saw the muzzle of the gun prodding his stomach, and dropped his right hand to his side.

'Get outa here,' Manning rasped. 'I can't stand the sight of blood on an empty stomach.'

'I got the feeling you are the guy I'm watching for.' Jackson backed off a couple of steps. 'I'll see you later, when you get through eating.' He turned on his heel and headed for the batwings, and two of the three men sitting at the card table arose and followed him out, their spurs tinkling on the hard pine floor.

Manning watched the door until the trio had disappeared, then holstered his gun. The tender was standing tensely at the far end of the bar, and came forward slowly when he met Manning's harsh gaze, careful to keep his hands in sight.

'What was that all about?' he demanded. 'You sure got Jackson all fired up!'

'I was hoping mebbe you could tell me.' Manning wiped his lips on the back of his left hand. 'Who is Keno Jackson?'

'Gun boss for Dallas Thorpe, who owns Slashed T, the biggest spread on this range. Thorpe has been running roughshod over the local range for more than twenty years. He's got a crew of fifteen cowhands and ten gunnies on his payroll, of which Jackson is the ramrod, and them hellions have a bad habit of making life unbearable for their neighbours. The smaller ranchers that ain't dead are pulling stakes, scared into selling out to Thorpe.'

'Who's Manning? Jackson said he's watching for him to show.'

'A local rancher, Mort Manning, died about three months ago and left his spread to his nephew, who ain't turned up yet to collect. Jackson figgers to pull him up short and scare him into selling to Thorpe.' The tender turned when a woman called him, and Manning watched a Mexican girl set a laden plate on a nearby table. 'Your grub is ready, mister,' the tender said. 'You better enjoy it before Jackson comes nosing around again. And if you are the man Jackson is looking for then you got more than grub on your plate.

You got a helluva load of trouble.'

'Thanks for the information.' Manning took his rifle and saddle-bags across to the table and sat down, his thoughts mulling over the news he had gleaned. He removed his hat and began to eat with the enjoyment of one who had been too long on the trail. The food was good; boiled beef and potatoes, but he was unable to fully enjoy the meal for trouble was looming and he could not keep his mind from dwelling upon it.

By the time he had eaten his fill the saloon was becoming busy, and he was aware of many glances thrown in his direction. He rolled a smoke and tried to relax, then pulled out a letter which he had received in Mexico. When he had heard of his uncle's death he wrote to one Sam Askew, attorney at law here in Oaktown, laying claim to the Double M, and Askew had advised him to ride north immediately to settle the business. But there had been no mention of the situation as outlined by the bartender.

He took up his rifle and saddle-bags and left the saloon. The evening was well advanced now and shadows were beginning to crawl into the dusty corners of the town. Pausing on the side-walk he glanced around, his right hand resting on the butt of his holstered sixgun. He was hair-triggered for trouble but Jackson and his two pards were not in sight and he noted that their horses were gone from the hitching rail.

He walked along the sidewalk to the hotel and rented a room. When he had cleaned his sixgun and washed up he donned his store suit, dusted his hat and wiped his boots, then pinned his Ranger badge to his shirt under his jacket before venturing out into the town. He stood in the shadows on the sidewalk looking around, trying to gauge the tempo of this little town.

There was not much to see. A hot breeze was blowing in from the range and the dark sky was strewn with bright stars. Music was emanating from the saloon where he had eaten. A number of saddle horses were tied to various hitchrails along the street, and there were dark figures moving along the sidewalks on either side of the wide, rutted thoroughfare.

Manning made a round of the street, walking along one side to the outskirts before crossing over to check the other. He made a note of the various places of business, passing a bank and then the law office and jail. When he saw a sign on a door advertising Samuel Askew, attorney at law, and spotted a light in the office, he knocked at the door and entered to find a fleshy-faced, middle-aged man seated at a paper-strewn desk, intent upon an open file. There were shelves filled with ledgers and files, and on the wall beyond the desk was a large-scale map of Clearwater County.

'Heck, I'm closed!' the man snapped without looking up. 'If you got business with me then call again in the morning.

I got a load of work to catch up on.'

'I've ridden a long way to see you.' Manning spoke softly. He gave his name and produced the letter Askew had sent him.

The man scanned the letter then looked up into Manning's intent face. He sighed heavily and made a visible effort to relax. 'Howdy?' he greeted. 'I'm Sam Askew. So you're Chuck Manning! You ever been in this neck of the woods before?'

'No.' Manning shook his head. 'Uncle Mort drifted south from Kansas after the war and bought the Double M. I ain't seen him since I was a kid. And he wasn't so very old. What did he die of?'

'Greed, I reckon! Someone wanted to get ahold of the Double M, and when Mort wouldn't sell out he was shot in the back.'

'Murdered!' Manning's expression hardened. 'You didn't put that in your letter.'

'Figured it would be better to give

you the whole story when you arrived.' Askew's blue eyes were filled with determination. He sagged in his seat and loosened the tie around his thick neck.

'Before you say anything more I better tell you that I had a run-in with a galoot named Keno Jackson soon as I hit town.' Manning clenched his hands at the recollection and mentally vowed to take up the matter with Jackson when next they met.

'The hell you say! Heck, I didn't hear no shooting.'

'It didn't go that far.' Manning explained what had occurred, and mentioned what he had learned from the bartender afterwards.

Askew nodded, pulling at his long nose. 'I reckon you don't have to look past Dallas Thorpe's gunslicks to find out who killed your uncle, but I don't figure you'll be able to prove it. And if you take over the Double M you won't have a prayer unless you back yourself with a crew of gunnies.'

'What has the law done about this situation?'

Askew laughed mirthlessly. 'Wait till you meet our local lawman. Deputy Sheriff Charlie Aitken was given a tin star because although he's a hardcase, he's a useless sonofabitch with no interest in the job. The county sheriff, Ben Gauvin, has an office in San Lorenzo, forty-miles to the east, and you won't see him in these parts very often. Comes around mebbe a couple of times a year or sends his chief deputy, who ain't much better than Aitken.'

'So Thorpe sits the big saddle around here and rules the roost, huh?' Manning nodded. 'I get the picture.'

'You better get it right, because the minute your identity is known your life won't be worth a plugged nickel.'

Manning recalled Jackson's arrogant manner and knew the lawyer was not exaggerating. 'Is anyone out at Double M taking care of the place?' he asked. 'Did Mort have a crew? Is it a big spread? I got no idea what's out there.'

'About ten thousand acres lies under the Double M brand, and your uncle was running some seven thousand head at the time he was killed.' Askew shook his head. 'There's a lot of rustling going on around the range, and most of it, I've heard, is done by Thorpe's crew. That bunch ain't past burning out some rancher who makes a stand against Slashed T. It's happened several times in the past. And since your uncle died some of his fences have been pulled down and Slashed T cattle are grazing on your grass. As to crew, Mort had a dozen men backing him, but they drifted when he died. I put in a watchman to keep an eye on the place. Old Hank Tupp. He's living out there with his granddaughter, and the last time I saw Tupp he was complaining about the night riders and the threats he's been getting.'

Manning remained silent for a spell, his thoughts drifting, and Askew watched him intently.

'Ain't much of a prospect, huh?' the lawyer asked at length. 'I want you to sign some papers that will make the spread legally yours, but I figure it'll be like signing your death warrant. The minute Thorpe learns who you are he'll set his gunnies against you. I don't see a way out for you, unless you sell to Thorpe at his price.'

'I ain't of a mind to do that.' Manning shook his head. 'And Jackson is here in town with a couple of sidekicks, already looking for me. So Thorpe knows I'm coming, huh?'

'It's common knowledge hereabouts.' Askew grimaced. 'The whole-danged county is waiting for you to show.'

'I'm handy with a gun, but not that handy.' Manning rasped long fingers through the dark stubble on his chin. 'I've been riding with the Texas Rangers for the last four years, and I got leave of absence to tidy up my personal affairs around here. I also have to check out the reports of lawlessness in this county that have been drifting into Ranger headquarters in Houston.'

'Do you know Captain Truscott?'

'I'm in his Company.'

'Then contact him. You can't handle this trouble on your own. Truscott needs to send a couple of men in here to help.'

'I'll look around some before deciding what to do. You got some papers for me to sign?'

'Yeah.' Askew got up from the desk and took down a file from the shelf. He sat down again and opened the file. Manning watched him for some moments, and then Askew passed over a thin sheaf of papers. 'Read them, initial each page, and sign your full name at the bottom of the last page,' he instructed.

Manning complied, and sighed heavily when he signed the last page, which was a receipt and discharged Askew from all further responsibility.

Askew nodded. 'I'll continue to act for you, if you wish. I guess there will be some legal business from time to time.' He glanced at a clock on the back wall. 'I figure you'll need to check the ranch account at the bank and change it to your own name. If we leave now we might just catch Adam Shreeve, the banker, before he closes his office. You'll need to be introduced to him so he'll know you by sight. Then you'll be on your own'

'It can wait until morning.' Manning shrugged. 'I ain't in a hurry to pin myself down to the Double M.'

'Can't say I blame you, but I'd like to get shot of the worry of being responsible for the place. Take over the ranch officially and we can start afresh. And it might be better to let it be known that you're a Ranger. It could be a lot safer than admitting your real identity.'

Manning nodded and Askew arose and put on his coat. They left the office and walked through the soft darkness of the evening to the bank. Manning saw a light inside the building, and Askew, leading the way to a side door, knocked insistently. They waited in the shadows until a voice demanded their identity. Askew replied and the door was opened to admit them.

Adam Shreeve was a stocky man, fleshy from lack of exercise, and with an intangible air of prosperity about him. He was about fifty, Manning judged, and his deep set blue eyes were lined from years of close paperwork. His dome-shaped head was completely bald. He shook hands with Manning, his grip firm and reassuring.

'I can see you resemble your uncle,' he observed. 'It was a great shock to everyone when Mort was found dead. I hope you'll fare better when you take over the Double M.'

'Can I leave you now?' Askew cut in. 'I've got a lot of work on hand before the circuit judge arrives next week. We've settled the legal business of the take-over and you don't need me for the financial details.' He held out his hand to Manning. 'Good luck for the future. You know where to find me should you need me for anything, and don't hesitate to look me up if you do get problems. If anyone asks, I'll say Chuck Manning hasn't showed up yet.'

'Thanks.' Manning's face was grim. 'I expect I'll see you again in the near future.'

Askew nodded and departed, and Shreeve consulted a gold pocket watch. 'We could settle your business now,' he said. 'All I need is your signature and you can take over your uncle's account. I expect you're impatient to get out to the ranch.'

'No.' Manning shook his head. 'I hear there's trouble on the range, and my uncle was murdered. I'm gonna have to look into that, both as a Texas Ranger and as the new owner of Double M, and I need to protect myself before I step into my uncle's boots.'

'You won't have far to look for those responsible for the trouble.' Shreeve spoke grimly. 'It's not for me to name anyone, but I guess you'll soon work out who your enemies are. Sit down and I'll get the account. When I have your signature as a specimen you'll be in business.'

Manning sat down, and his thoughts were harsh as he handled the business needed to conclude his take-over of the Double M. There was obviously more trouble around here than he could handle, and he would be a fool to attempt anything alone. But if he hired a crew he would need a small army to combat those who were determined to control the local range, and resistance was the only way he could hope to survive, for it was obvious that whoever was behind the trouble would want him dead at the earliest opportunity.

2

When Manning left the bank he was richer by a bank balance of some $15,000, but his thoughts were harsh as he walked along the shadowy street towards the law office. His uncle had been murdered, and something would be have to be done about that, but first he had to discover the identity of the killer.

He paused on the sidewalk and turned slowly to study the darkened street, which had lanterns burning at intervals along its length, forming pools of yellow glare in the impenetrable night. Music was coming from the saloon about halfway along the street on the left, and he heard the clop of hooves as a rider came into town from the range. He saw a shadow cross the sidewalk and enter the saloon, and for a moment he was aware of loneliness tugging inside his breast.

He struggled with unaccustomed emotion as he turned and continued towards the law office, which had lamplight spilling through the big window on the far side of the heavy wooden door. The light cast a large oblong of brilliance across the sidewalk and over the rutted dust of the street in front of it, and beyond it the darkness was black and solid.

Stepping foward, Manning reached out his left hand to open the door, but at that moment he heard a scraping sound from the far corner of the office, beyond the impenetrable bar of light issuing from the big window. The sound alerted him and he dropped his right hand to the butt of his gun.

Manning narrowed his eyes as he peered into the brilliance. Then he heard the ominous sound of a sixgun being cocked and hurled himself to the right, towards the wall of the law office. The breath was knocked out of him by his impact with hard adobe bricks and he fell to the ground in a heap, dimly aware of shots smashing the silence and the crackle of closely passing slugs barely missing him.

His eyes were dazzled by the light and he eased on to his left side, reaching for the butt of his holstered gun. Echoes were racketing around the street, fading slowly, and he cocked his gun and remained motionless. He picked up the sound of running feet somewhere in the background and eased to one knee, his lips compressed and his eyes narrowed. Then he heard the sudden clatter of hooves, which receded quickly, and slowly regained his feet.

The law office door was suddenly dragged open, permitting yet more light to bathe the street, and Manning holstered his gun as a big figure stepped squarely into the doorway.

'What in hell is goin' on?' a man demanded hoarsely. He half turned to confront Manning, a star on his vest front glinting in the lamplight. He was almost as big as Manning, and there was a spiteful twist to his thin lips. He was holding a cocked sixgun in his right hand, the muzzle pointing directly at Manning's chest. 'What was that shootin' about?'

'You'd better ask the man who did it,' countered Manning. 'He was beyond the light of your window, and I heard him riding off over the back lot before you opened the door.'

'Was you the target?' The deputy came out of the doorway, his gun muzzle unwavering in its aim at Manning's chest. 'Heck, you're a stranger! What was the shooting about?'

'I might be able to tell you one day, if I live long enough to find out, and if you're interested.'

The man grinned meanly and waggled his gun. 'Step into the office. I wanta get to the bottom of this. You're a stranger, and I reckon you must have brought trouble with you. Well, that don't sit too well with me. I'm Charlie Aitken, deputy sheriff. I handle the law in this county. Keep your hand away from your gun and don't try to be smart. No one around here is smarter than me. I'm gonna check you out, mister, and I'll throw you in jail if I don't like what I find.'

Manning grimaced and went forward slowly while Aitken backed into the office. Manning kicked the door to with his left foot, aware that Aitken's gun was still covering him. Manning paused on the threshold, absorbing the rough aggression of the deputy.

'There were three shots,' rasped Aitken, 'and I wanta know who fired 'em?'

'I got no idea.' Manning shrugged impatiently, able to see the kind of lawman Aitken was. 'Check my gun, if it's not too much trouble. It's clean. What kind of law do you run around here? I get shot at and you hold me on the end of a gun.'

'I'll ask the questions.' Aitken's thick tone was harsh and bullying. 'Were the shots fired at you?'

'Seeing that they didn't miss me by more than an inch, I'd say they were.'

'You had trouble on your way to town?'

'No.' Manning snapped the word and fell silent, aware that he instinctively disliked Aitken. The man had an air about him that warned Manning to be careful. 'Someone braced me the minute I got into town though. Name of Keno Jackson.' He explained what had occurred in the saloon.

'Uhuh!' Aitken's pale eyes glinted. 'There's been talk that the Slashed T are on the look-out for the new owner of the Double M, who's due to ride in any time now. Are you the guy?'

'Nope. I heard they're looking for a guy named Manning.'

'Yeah, and I wouldn't wanta be in his boots for a year's pay.' Aitken chuckled hoarsely. He was probably thirty years old, fleshy, with porcine features — piggish eyes and a flattish nose. 'If he figures to come in here and take over the Double M then he better think again.'

'Hasn't he got a legal right to the spread?'

'I guess so, if Sam Askew sent for him.' Aitken's eyes were glinting like blue windswept ice. 'And if Dallas Thorpe has taken a fancy to the Double M then no Johnny-come-lately is gonna walk in and inherit it.'

'What happens if Manning comes to you for protection?'

'What do you figger I could do; me, a man alone? I wouldn't be able to raise a posse. No one in the whole-danged county would step out of line against Slashed T.' Aitken slowly holstered his gun. 'Anyway, I get my orders from Sheriff Gauvin. He bosses the law in the county.'

'And he's told you to walk wide around Slashed T, huh?' Manning nodded. 'That figures.'

'He ain't said that at all. And what's it to you?' Aitken's heavy features hardened. 'You're asking too many damn questions, mister. Who are you and what's your business in town? You got any visible means of support?' He half eased his gun out of its holster. 'I don't want no trouble-makers around here, see. If you're bent on causing trouble then I'll dump you in a cell and throw away the key.'

'But Slashed T can cause any trouble they like, huh? Sounds like they already committed murder and got away with it. Is that the kind of law you run?'

'Why you — !' Aitken tried to finish his draw, his slitted blue eyes blazing with sudden fury. But his gun had not cleared leather when Manning blocked the draw with his left hand and whirled his right fist in a tight arc to land a solid punch against his stubbled jaw. Aitken's head snapped sideways and he uttered a thin yell of shock as he sprawled backwards to fall upon his desk before rolling off and crashing to the floor behind it. Manning followed closely, ready for further action.

But Aitken was out cold. His gun was

lying at his side and his arms were outflung. Manning kicked the sixgun into a corner, and as he bent over the motionless deputy the street door was thrust open and a man came bustling in to pause on the threshold and gaze at Manning. He was unable to see Aitken lying behind the desk, and frowned.

'You're a stranger,' gasped the newcomer. Breathless, he leaned against the doorpost, his chest heaving while he tried to regain his breath. 'I got a bad habit of running when I hear gunshots. Ain't you the guy the Slashed T hard-cases are waiting for? Where's Aitken?'

Manning motioned towards the back of the desk and the man craned forward until he could see the motionless figure of the deputy. The newcomer was tall and thin, in his fifties, and was wearing a store suit of good cloth and a flat-crowned hat. He backed off, his eyes widening.

'Is he dead?' he demanded.

'No. Just out cold.' Manning smiled.

'He mistook me for someone else and tried to pull his gun. I had to hit him to prevent bloodshed.'

'Then you better get outa here before he comes to, and if you got any sense you'll spread leather until you're clear of the county.'

'I can't do that. I got business around here.' Manning saw that Aitken was stirring and reached down to secure a grip on the deputy's shirt. He lifted the big man easily and dumped him in the seat behind the desk, holding him in place with a powerful left hand and slapping his face lightly with his right.

The newcomer came around the desk and dragged open a drawer. He took out a half-filled whisky bottle and uncorked it.

'This'll bring him round.' He stuck the neck of the bottle between the deputy's teeth.

Aitken swallowed some of the liquor and half-choked before the bottle was removed. Manning backed off and stood waiting. The newcomer looked up at him, still shaking his head.

'You better not let him get hold of a gun when he's on his feet' he advised, 'or you'll have to kill him. I'm Doc Hoyt, by the way. I'm generally kept too busy these days, tending to bullet wounds and the like, and I don't fancy having to work on you right now. It's too near supper-time. Won't you leave while the going is good?'

'Aitken won't give me any trouble.' Manning pushed aside his jacket to reveal the law badge pinned to his shirt front: a small silver star set in a silver circle.

'You're a Ranger!' Doc Hoyt grinned. 'Now that's really something.' He stepped back as Aitken lumbered up out of the chair and reeled sideways to the wall, propping himself against it while shaking his head, his eyelids flickering rapidly. Then he straightened slowly and opened his eyes fully, his gaze filling with hatred and fury as he looked at Manning. His right hand slapped his holster but stopped when he realized his gun was not in place.

'Hold it right there, Charlie.' There was a half-smile on Hoyt's lips, and he winked at the watchful Manning. 'You're way out of line this time. This man is a Ranger!'

Aitken blinked, his features freezing into disbelief, and Manning pulled aside his jacket to reveal his badge.

'You didn't give me time to introduce myself,' he said, 'and when you started to pull your gun there was only one way to prevent bloodshed.'

'Why in hell ain't you got that badge pinned outside your coat?' Aitken snarled.

'Because it makes too good a target.' Manning's tone was low-pitched, unemotional. 'And you didn't have to go off half-cocked. Who taught you law business?'

'I've had a lot of trouble around here. It's got so a man can't take chances.' Aitken frowned. 'Are you here on Ranger business?'

'I've been told to take a look around.

The sheriff in San Lorenzo has been informed that I'm coming into the county.'

'But I ain't been told.' Aitken shook his head. 'It's a helluva way to run the law.'

'What can you tell me about the trouble involving Double M?' Manning's tone was crisp and his gaze held the deputy's eyes, gauging the temper of the man.

'Not much.' Aitken shook his head slowly, trying to gather his thoughts. 'Mort Manning was found shot in the back out by Water Valley, where his spread is at. He'd complained of rustling and night riders disturbing his peace. I looked around and found plenty of tracks but couldn't find out who made them. When Manning was killed I heard he had a nephew who was coming in to take over the ranch. I've been keeping a lookout for the nephew but ain't seen hide nor hair of him yet.'

'And Slashed T has men in town awaiting the arrival of the new owner.'

Manning set his teeth into his bottom lip. 'I was braced by Keno Jackson when I showed up. He's figuring to push Manning into a gunfight and kill him, huh? Is that how it reads?'

Aitken shrugged. 'You'll have to ask Jackson about that. There's nothing I can do until lead starts flying.'

'And someone took a couple of shots at me from the corner of your office! It looks like I'm pegged as the new owner of Double M.' Manning lifted his left hand and touched the badge under his jacket.

'You'll have to take that up with Dallas Thorpe hisself.' Aitken shrugged his heavy shoulders. 'He's in the big saddle, and figgers he's above the law. But make the mistake of riding out to Slashed T to see Thorpe and you'll pay for it with your life, Ranger or not.'

Manning moved to the door. He glanced at the silent doctor. 'Nice to meet you, Doc,' he said. 'See you around, huh?'

'Sure.' Hoyt nodded. 'But you'd

better be on your guard the minute you step outa that door. There'll be a number of Slashed T gunnies on the watch for Manning, and any stranger is sure to be taken for him. Life is cheap in this county.'

Manning nodded and departed. He closed the office door and stood in the shadows, looking around the deserted street. Silence had closed in around him like a brooding threat, and for a moment he savoured it, aware that the very nature of his way of life had rendered him friendless, a lonely man in a hostile country where badmen were ready to shoot him on sight and law-abiding men regarded him with suspicion.

A hunch struck him and he opened the door again. Aitken's head swivelled quickly, and the deputy glared at him. Manning entered and picked up the nearer of the two lanterns illuminating the office.

'I wanta take a look at the spot those shots were fired from,' he said, and Doc

Hoyt joined him as he went out.

They walked to the left-hand corner of the building and Manning found himself looking into a narrow alley. He squatted at the corner, holding the lantern aloft, and looked at the hard packed earth of the alley.

'Ground is too hard to take sign,' observed the doc.

'Whoever he was, he left on a horse,' Manning mused. 'I heard him riding away.' He walked farther into the alley, finding the ground a little softer, and spotted fresh hoofprints. But they told him nothing and he shook his head. It looked as if he would have to handle this business the hard way.

He gave the lamp to Hoyt, who went back into the law office, and went along the sidewalk towards the saloon, aware that this particular case was fraught with extra danger because he had a personal interest in the outcome. The saloon was busy, he discovered when he glanced in over the batwings, and stood for a moment checking the score or so occupants. When he saw Keno Jackson sitting in on a card game at one of the tables his eyes narrowed and he drew a deep breath. There was no point in postponing the inevitable, he decided, and eased his gun in its holster as he shouldered through the swing doors and walked to Jackson's table.

The card player facing Manning as he casually approached the table spoke urgently to Jackson, who was seated to the left, his right side to Manning. The Slashed T ramrod glanced up and tensed as Manning's big figure loomed over him and, as Manning halted beside him, he dropped his right hand to the butt of his holstered gun.

'Try to draw that gun and I'll stuff the muzzle down your throat,' Manning snapped. Silence fell as his loud voice reached out. Men paused, and as soon as the situation was read by those nearest the table there was a general exodus from the spot.

'You braced me earlier,' Manning continued, 'and when I went along the street I was shot at by a sneaking ambusher. I figure someone was acting on your orders, Jackson, so name him. I got business with him, this time face to face.'

Jackson was at a disadvantage with Manning standing so close to his right side. He was tight-lipped. Manning had seen arrogance in him at their first meeting, and pointers in his manner that indicated a fiery temper. Manning's sharp tone put a dull colour into the ramrod's leathery cheeks and set a glint of flame sparkling in his eyes.

'Get the hell outa here before you wind up on boot hill,' Jackson snarled, the fingers of his right hand clenching around the butt of his holstered gun.

'Somebody's already tried to put me there and made the mistake of failing.' Manning's knees bent a little and his shoulders flexed. 'You figure you can do it?'

Men moved quickly away from the card table. Chairs scraped as gun-wise men hurried to put distance between themselves and trouble. A red flame was flickering in Jackson's pale eyes and he thrust himself to his feet in a single, powerful movement, sending his chair crashing over backwards. Manning backed off a couple of swift steps, his tall figure seemingly at ease, his right hand down at his side, the butt of his holstered sixgun touching the inside of his right wrist. He had it figured that Jackson had to be the toughest gun hand on the Slashed T payroll, and that if he beat the ramrod now, Thorpe's gun crew would be practically leaderless.

'Mister, you sure are determined to commit suicide.' Jackson ground out the words as if they were burning his mouth. 'But talk is cheap. Turn your gunhand loose and we'll see if you can back up your words.'

'You're doing the talking. You start it.' Manning grinned mockingly.

Jackson seemed to freeze in his stance, and a tense silence closed in around them. Then the ramrod set his right hand in motion, and he was fast. He grasped the butt of his gun, his thumb easing back the hammer as he lifted the weapon clear of leather. Then he froze, for Manning's sixgun was levelled at him, cocked and ready for action while he still had to level his own weapon.

'It looks like you ain't in my class,' Manning observed. 'If you wanta try it again then slide your gun back into leather and make another play. But next time I'll shoot. If you still fancy your chance then turn her loose.'

Jackson thrust his gun deep into its holster and eased the trigger forward. His hand tremored as he let go of the butt in token of surrender. His face was expressionless but he was shaken. If he had beaten this stranger to the draw he would have shot him down without compunction. But the speed of Manning's draw brought home to him how close to death he had been, and an icy sweat had turned his brow clammy and his courage and nerve seemed to ooze out of his sweaty pores.

'You wanta try with your fists?' Manning offered. 'It looks like you're anxious to prove yourself, and I'd rather fight now than run the risk of having you come up on me from behind.'

An ugly snarl twitched Jackson's lips and his sudden grin was filled with wicked jubilation. 'You sonofabitch!' he grated. 'You got a big mouth, and you've talked yourself into the whipping of your life.'

Manning reholstered his gun and clenched his big hands. His narrowed eyes took on a dread look. Muscles stood out along his jawline. A deepening of the tension gripped those present in the saloon, and a deathly silence spread quickly.

Jackson darted forward in a rush, his fists swinging, his weight on his toes as he leaned into the attack. His footwork brought him in close. His powerful shoulders were hunched and his hands clenched into punishing clubs.

Instead of fading before the rush, Manning stepped forward a half-pace, his hands clenched into fists and lifting. Jackson loosed a powerful left and Manning took it on his right shoulder, jerking his own left into an uppercut that smacked solidly against the ramrod's unprotected chin. Jackson halted as if he had run into the side of a barn and Manning's right whipped across and made contact with the side of the man's jaw. The sound of the blows echoed in the tense silence, and Jackson stiffened, his hands falling helplessly to his sides. His face looked stricken, as if he had been pole-axed. Then he dropped to the floor, raising a puff of sawdust, and lay inert, breathing stertorously, his heavy chest rising and falling irregularly.

Manning looked at the other men seated at the table. They were staring at him as if mesmerized, unable to accept the swift downfall of their ranch boss. Manning moved away a couple of paces.

'If any of you ride with Jackson then get up and take him outa here.' Manning spoke sharply. 'Take him back to the Slashed T, and tell Dallas Thorpe to pull in his horns. I'm a Texas Ranger, and I'm in the county to look at the trouble that's boiling over. Now get outa here and keep on going.'

Two of the men arose immediately and lifted Jackson out of the sawdust. Nobody else moved as the unconscious ramrod was borne away, and it was not until the batwings flapped behind the departing figures that men began breathing normally again.

Manning heaved a long sigh and narrowed his eyes. It had been easy to make a bold start against Slashed T, but it would be a horse of another colour to continue successfully in the same vein and he knew it. No matter what he did, the future looked bleak, and when it came inevitably to the ultimate test of strength he would undoubtedly be found wanting. The fact that he had the law on his side would not count for much when the chips went down. But the knowledge that he might lose out in the end did not unduly worry him.

3

Manning had a beer while he considered the situation. He did not want to complicate his investigation by combining his duty as a Ranger with a personal hunt for whoever had killed his uncle. The Double M had to take second place despite his connection with it. Duty had to come first, and although he suspected the Slashed T of being responsible for his uncle's death he would pursue his enquiries along the accepted methods of investigation as detailed by his superiors, until he had proof enough to act.

Thinking of the shots that had been fired at him from the corner of the jail, he was certain that it had been done by those who wanted to prevent Manning from taking over the Double M, and, as far as he was aware, only two men in town knew he was Chuck Manning

— Askew the lawyer and Shreeve the banker. Had either of them passed on the news that he was Mort Manning's nephew?

He finished his beer and started towards the batwings, and was twenty feet from the threshold when the swing doors were thrust open and a tall, big-boned man of about fifty entered. He paused on the threshold, and Manning walked towards him, his keen gaze taking in the newcomer's appearance. Dark features were pinched, brown eyes narrowed from the habit of peering across the wide, sun-drenched range. He was tall and wide-shouldered, but gaunted like a man too familiar with a jolting saddle. He was wearing good quality range clothes: a leather vest over a dull grey shirt, blue pants and brown leather riding boots. His grey Stetson was pulled forward so that the down-turned brim shielded his restless eyes.

'I hear there's a Ranger in town.' His harsh voice crackled in the silence that acknowledged his arrival.

'You're facing him,' Manning spoke quietly, pushing aside his vest to briefly reveal the law badge pinned to his shirt. 'Who are you and what's on your mind, mister?' As he spoke he noted a couple of faces outside the batwings, peering intently into the saloon, and then the swing doors were pushed inwards and two men entered to stand, tense and alert, behind the newcomer.

'I'm Dallas Thorpe. I own Slashed T.'

'Glad to meet you, Thorpe.' Manning nodded briefly. 'You've saved me a ride. I was coming out to your place in the morning to talk with you.'

'I hear you've had trouble with my ramrod, Keno Jackson.' The rancher's tone was sharp. 'I can't believe a Ranger would start trouble, and it ain't like Jackson to go on the prod, especially against the law.'

'I didn't have any trouble handling him. I figure he thought I was someone else.' There was a glint far back in Manning's brown eyes. 'It seems a man called Manning is expected to ride in at any time, and he's of special interest to you.'

'Jackson's obviously got hold of the wrong end of the stick.' Thorpe's eyes were narrowed, his gaze darkly intent as he studied Manning's face. 'You wanta sit down and talk?'

'Sure thing. I always prefer talk to action, and it'll save me a ride. I figure to be around town for a spell.' Manning turned and went to a corner table.

Thorpe followed him, and the two men at the rancher's back relaxed and moved to the bar.

'Tender, bring over a bottle of your best whisky and a couple glasses,' Thorpe ordered. He seated himself opposite Manning and removed his hat to reveal iron-grey hair that was short and tightly waved.

'Well, what's on your mind?' he demanded.

'I heard tell you're scaring smaller ranchers and buying them out cheap.'

Thorpe cursed and shook his head.

'There's always that kind of talk about a big rancher,' he snapped, 'and I'm the biggest in the county. You're gonna have to do better than that to get to the bottom of the trouble on this range.'

'I mean to do better.' Manning smiled.

'You need to hear the other side of the story before you decide who's to blame for what's going on around here.' Thorpe paused and took a bottle of whisky and two glasses from the tender who approached. 'I have to run a big crew of gunnies beside my range hands to protect what I've got. I've been hit by rustlers more times than I can count, and suffered considerable losses. No one's mentioned that to you, huh?'

'Have you reported the facts to the local law?'

Thorpe made a noise of disgust. 'The local law! Hell, why would I waste my time trying that? Have you met Charlie Aitken? He's a slob with no interest in law dealing.'

'He's only a deputy. There's a sheriff

in San Lorenzo.'

'You wanta talk to him before you do anything else. Then you'll see what I'm up against.' Thorpe poured whisky liberally into the two glasses and recorked the bottle. He picked up a glass and motioned towards the other, holding Manning's gaze. 'Here's to the law doing something about the crooked men in the county. I don't know what you hope to do, but any time you need gun help you only got to ask and my crew will be ready to back you. I can't say fairer than that. I'm ready to do my bit for law and order.'

'Thanks.' Manning nodded. 'You got any idea who's behind the trouble?'

'If I knew that there wouldn't be a job here for you. I'd have handled it myself, like we used to in the old days.'

'What happened to Mort Manning?'

'I don't know. I heard he'd been found dry-gulched, which is a way of death that's become too popular in these parts of late.'

'Is that why there's a couple of

gunnies shadowing you?'

Thorpe shrugged. 'I ain't taking any chances, the situation being what it is.'

'Why was Jackson waiting in town with a couple of your gunhands for the new owner of Double M to show up? Jackson was on the prod when I arrived. If I had been Manning there would have been gunplay.'

'Jackson must have misunderstood my orders. He was here to get to Manning before anyone could kill him. Whoever killed his uncle will have to remove him too.'

'I guess so, but I don't figure to sit around waiting for the man to turn up.' Manning did not touch the drink Thorpe had poured for him. He watched the rancher pour another three fingers of rye whisky into his own glass and drink it at a gulp.

'You ain't drinking with me,' Thorpe suddenly accused. 'Do you figure I'm guilty, like everyone says?'

'I don't pay heed to hearsay.' Manning shook his head. 'I'll gather my own evidence, and when I have the deadwood on the guilty man I'll act. But you better put a curb on your gunhands. They've been making wide tracks around the county, and it's got to stop.'

'I'll deal with it.' Thorpe put on his hat, thrust back his chair and got to his feet. He paused, gazing down at Manning, then reached across the table and picked up Manning's glass. Drinking the contents at a gulp, he grinned and slammed the glass back on the table. 'I'll buy you a drink when you can believe that I'm innocent,' he rasped, and turned on his heel and departed, followed by his gunhands.

Manning shook his head as he considered. Someone was running the lawlessness, and if it was not Thorpe then another badman was deeply buried in the background and would have to be flushed out. He got to his feet and walked to the door, slipping out to stand in the shadows with his back to the front wall of the saloon. A cool breeze fanned his face and he drew a deep breath.

Keno Jackson had been intent on killing the new owner of the Double M ranch whenever he appeared. But on whose orders was the Slashed T ramrod acting? Thorpe was maintaining an appearance of innocence, but apparently Jackson had been been hanging around town for days, waiting for any stranger to arrive, and he could not have wasted his time in that manner without Thorpe's approval.

Keeping to the shadows, Manning made his way along the sidewalk to the hotel. As he entered, the two gunhands who had taken Jackson from the saloon came down the stairs and went into the small hotel bar. Manning glanced into the bar. Thorpe was seated at a corner table with two men and was talking earnestly. Manning turned to cross to the desk to speak to the clerk.

'Is Keno Jackson in the hotel?' he demanded.

The clerk, an old man with white hair

and a grey beard, shook his head slowly.

'I've just come on duty, mister.'

'Then check the register.' Manning eased aside his vest to reveal his Ranger badge. 'I'm on law business.'

'I heard a Ranger had showed up.' The clerk studied the hotel register. 'You're the man, huh?' He glanced up at Manning, who nodded. 'Yeah.' He shook his head slowly. 'Well Jackson is in the room next to yours. You sure worked him over, but now you got to watch your back.'

Manning nodded. 'Thanks for the information. You got an opinion of who is behind the trouble in this county?'

'Me?' The old man shook his head. 'I'm seventy, and I got to my age by keeping my eyes open and my mouth shut. I ain't about to change my way of life now. If you wanta know anything about the goings on in this county then you should go talk to Reuben Nash. He owns the *Clarion*, and all you need to do is look up the back numbers of his newspaper to get the whole tale. The

Clarion's head office is in San Lorenzo, but there's a small office in town, just along the street.'

'Thanks. I guess the office won't be open now.'

'Jed Petrie runs it, and he sleeps in a back room there. You could find him tonight, if it's urgent.'

'Thanks.' Manning left the hotel and moved into the dense shadows along the sidewalk. He eased through the darkness towards the law office. If anyone knew anything at all about the situation in this county it would be the deputy sheriff. But the man's appearance and attitude did not promote confidence in Manning. Aitken seemed to be a poor type of lawman.

Hooves sounded along the street, coming from out of town, and their rapid beating alerted Manning to trouble. No one rode that fast at night unless it was a dire emergency. He was close to the law office, and noted that the big front window was filled with yellow lamplight. He went forward carefully, and was only yards from the office when a rider loomed up out of the impenetrable darkness and slewed the horse into a slithering halt. A slight figure sprang from the saddle, wrapped the reins around the hitching rail, and ran into the office. Manning followed only a couple of yards behind.

He was surprised, when he crossed the threshold of the office, to find the newcomer was female. Slight of build, and with yellowish hair showing under her small plains hat, she was breathless and distraught. Her voice was raised above its normal pitch and her words were uttered in a torrent as she clasped her hands together and wrung them.

Charlie Aitken was seated at his desk, chair tilted back, his feet upon the paper-strewn surface. His fleshy face was set in a brutish expression, his lips drawn into a tight, thin gash under his bulbous nose.

'Hey, leave the galloping to your hoss, Laura,' he cut in. 'I ain't getting a word of what you're saying. Start again and let me have it slow.' He spotted Manning's movement in the doorway and straightened, dropping his feet to the floor and pulling the chair closer to the desk. 'What was that you said about your pa?'

'He's been shot — dry-gulched!'

'Is he dead?' Aitken demanded.

'No. But he's hurt bad. I came in for Doc Hoyt, and ma said I had to let you know.'

'Where do you live?' cut in Manning.

The girl turned shocked eyes towards him. She was swaying, almost out on her feet, and Manning grasped her elbow and led her to a seat.

'Tented W.' She refused to sit down, filled with impatience and shock. 'I must tell the doctor. Pa was bleeding real bad when I left the ranch.'

'Aitken, tell Doc Hoyt to ride on out to Tented W soon as he can,' Manning rapped. 'I'll go out there to look around.'

'Who are you?' the girl asked as she hurried to the door.

Manning grasped her arm. 'I'm a Texas Ranger. Don't be in such a hurry. I doubt if your horse can carry you back to the ranch, the way you rode it in. We'll go along to the livery, get you a fresh mount and collect my horse. Let's go.'

He caught a glimpse of Aitken's face as he ushered the girl out into the darkness. The deputy was frowning, shaking his head. Manning gained the impression that Aitken was not pleased with the way he had taken over, and he nodded to himself as he caught up the reins of the girl's horse and led the way along the street towards the livery barn.

'What's your name, and where is Tented W?' Manning asked.

'I'm Laura Walton. Tented W is ten miles north-west of town.'

'That puts it somewhere close to Double M, huh?' Manning grimaced in the darkness. 'Looks like I got here none too soon. There's a killer loose in this county and he's keeping himself busy.'

'Mort Manning was killed a few months ago.' The girl's voice trembled. 'We've been on the watch for trouble ever since, but even so my pa was almost killed at sundown.'

'Can you tell me what happened?' Manning glanced around, watching their surroundings. There was a knot of men standing on the sidewalk in front of the hotel, as if word of the latest shooting had already spread through the town, and Manning caught a glimpse of Dallas Thorpe at the centre of the group.

'I'll talk to you when we're on the trail back to the ranch,' she said sharply. 'I wouldn't want word of what happened to get out yet.'

Manning nodded, and they were silent until they reached the barn. He quickly saddled his horse, and the stableman gave the girl another mount to ride. Within moments they were cantering back along the main street, and Manning, not seeing any kind of activity around the law office, reined aside and stepped down from his saddle.

Crossing the sidewalk, he thrust open the door of the office and peered inside. His teeth clicked together when he saw Aitken sitting at the desk, his feet once more on the untidy surface.

'Have you informed the doc yet?' he demanded.

'I sent the jailer to pass the word.' Aitken shrugged. 'Hoyt will be out at the ranch soon as he can make it.'

Manning departed, dissatisfied with Aitken's behaviour. He swung into his saddle, rode in beside the girl and they left town at a fast clip. There was a fat crescent moon giving sufficient light to the trail to enable them to make good time, and Manning waited for the girl to tell him of the events leading to her ride to town.

'It looks like Dallas Thorpe is behind our trouble,' she said finally. 'He's been pestering pa to sell out to him, and the trouble started when pa refused. Hardcases are riding our range. There's been rustling, some of our stock have been shot, and our fences have been cut in several places.'

'Did anyone on your spread recognize the trespassers?'

The girl shook her head. 'No, but that don't signify. The trouble didn't start until after Thorpe tried to buy us out, which is exactly what happened to Double M. I overheard Mort Manning telling my pa that Thorpe was trying to buy him out but he was not gonna sell, and the next thing we heard, Manning had been murdered. Now they've tried to kill my pa.'

'Did your pa talk to the local law about his troubles?

'He sure did, but Aitken said he couldn't do anything about it. After Mort Manning was killed, my pa wrote to the Ranger Headquarters in Houston to get something done, and they wrote back saying they were gonna send someone to take a look around.'

'And here I am.' Manning smiled tightly, then twisted in his saddle and looked around. He had been listening intently for suspicious sounds ever since they left town. The wind was sighing through the long grass and he was accustomed to it, but now he fancied he had heard the sound of distant hoofbeats. But there was total silence and he could not pick up anything definite.

'There was trouble for other ranchers before Mort Manning was killed,' the girl continued. 'My pa asked around, and in each case Thorpe tried to buy someone out.'

'But Thorpe didn't buy Double M, did he? I heard tell a nephew of Mort Manning was coming to take over the place.'

'I wish him luck, but he'll find trouble waiting when he does show.'

Manning was frowning, but not because of the girl's words. He twisted in his saddle again, straining his ears, and this time he heard the click of a steel-shod hoof against a stone.

'Someone's behind us,' he said

sharply. 'How far are we from your spread?'

'About five miles. Shall we make a run for it?'

'No.' Manning shook his head. 'It's better to face trouble than run from it. Ride on about fifty yards and wait for me. I'll brace who ever is on our back trail.'

'It could be the doc,' she warned.

'Yeah, and it might not be,' he responded grimly.

The girl went on. Silence quickly descended. Manning turned his horse about and sat motionless, right hand on the butt of his gun and eyes slitted to pierce the night. He strained his ears and caught the sounds of approaching hooves more clearly. There was more than one horse out there, and he eased his sixgun in its holster and pulled the brim of his Stetson lower over his eyes to cut out the moonlight.

Sitting motionless in the saddle, Manning waited stolidly, aware that he needed a good break in order to set his investigation rolling. If he was attacked, and could take a prisoner, he would soon get a line on the guilty men.

The hoofbeats drew nearer, and presently he saw three riders materializing out of the darkness, moving easily along the trail from town. They were silent, intent, as if having some definite object in mind. Manning waited until they were within earshot, then challenged them.

'Hold it right there,' he called. 'I'm a Texas Ranger. Declare yourselves.'

At the sound of his voice the trio halted momentarily in surprise, then separated quickly, two moving off in opposite directions as if to get around Manning's position. The centre rider ducked low in his saddle and spurred his horse forward, intent on riding Manning down. A reddish gun flash split the darkness and a bullet whined past Manning's left ear.

He waited no longer and stepped down out of his saddle, palming his Colt in his right hand and thumbing back the hammer. He threw down on the approaching rider, narrowing his eyes to make out details. When he fired the gun bucked against his palm, and powdersmoke blew into his face, its acrid taste stinging his throat and making his eyes water.

The approaching rider tumbled out of his saddle, thumped on the hard range, and lay still. The horse continued, galloping past Manning, who trailed his reins and moved away from his horse as the other two began shooting at him from wide angles. He dropped to one knee and cuffed back his Stetson. Sweat was running down his face and he drew a quick, steadying breath.

The rider on the left was angling in towards him, shooting fast. Manning levelled his gun, swung his arm to match the man's movement and speed, and fired, grunting in satisfaction when the rider was swept out of his saddle as if struck by a giant hand.

Getting to his feet, Manning looked

for the third rider, but the man had vanished, and there was just the faint sound of rapidly receding hooves in the direction taken by Laura Walton. Manning drew a deep breath and held it for a moment, then exhaled slowly and the tension left him. He listened to the fading echoes of the shooting, still fired up by the swift action. Then he sighed and reloaded his spent chambers.

He holstered his gun and prepared to check the men he had downed. Then he heard the sound of hooves coming from the same direction the three riders had appeared and drew his gun once more. A single rider materialized. Manning challenged him.

'Doc Hoyt,' came the reply. 'What was that shooting?'

'I was about to check.' Manning recognized the doc's voice. 'You better stay back until I've disarmed the two I put down. They could still be dangerous.'

He moved to the fallen rider on his

left, gun steady in his hand. He could see the dark figure of a man lying crumpled in the short grass and covered it, ready for sudden movement, but he reached the figure and saw that it was lying with arms outflung. A discarded sixgun was nearby, glinting in the moonlight. He dropped to one knee beside the man, felt for a heartbeat, and found no sign of life.

Grim-faced, Manning went to the second man to discover that he was also dead. He straightened and called in Hoyt. The doctor came up quickly. Dismounting, the doc bent over the nearest dead man, striking a match and holding it close to the inert features.

'Do you know him?' Manning was eager to learn the identity of the strangers.

'Never seen him before. Heck, I thought I knew everyone in the county. I'll take a look at the other one.'

Manning stood motionless, looking around, ears strained for sounds of the third man returning. But there was no suspicious sound on the wide range, and he shook his head slowly. This was not going to be a push-over. Strangers had been brought in to do some dirty work, and he knew without being told that he would not be able to trace them back to the man behind the trouble.

4

'You left town with Laura Walton.' Hoyt spoke softly, cutting into Manning's thoughts.

'Yeah. And when I heard these riders coming I told her to ride on ahead. There's no telling what she'll be thinking after hearing the shooting. We'd better get on. I'll clean up around here later.'

Manning went to his horse and swung into the saddle. The doc rode up beside him and they continued. Manning looked around, alert for more trouble because there was one rider unaccounted for. He gazed ahead, expecting to see the girl sitting her horse, but they travelled several hundred yards and there was no sign of her.

'I reckon she was spooked by the sound of shooting and high-tailed it home,' said Hoyt. 'I need to get to

Tented W fast, and there's nothing you can do out on the range at night. You're gonna have to wait up until morning whether you like it or not. So let's make tracks for Tented W.'

Manning gigged his mount and they travelled fast, the doc slightly in the lead and pointing the way. Eventually Manning saw lamplight in the distance, and Hoyt cleared his throat.

'That's Tented W,' he said.

They rode into the yard and a voice called out of the shadows of the nearby barn, demanding their identity. Hoyt replied and they continued to the house. The front door was opened as they reached the porch and yellow lamp light came spilling out across the dusty yard, chasing out the velvet darkness and creating heavy shadows beyond the porch.

'Laura, is that you?' a woman's voice demanded.

'It's Doc Hoyt, Martha, and I got a Texas Ranger with me. Ain't Laura come home?'

'She rode into town hours ago to fetch you.' The woman's voice tremored with fear. 'I haven't seen her since.'

Manning tightened his lips at the news. He had been hoping the girl had ridden for home when the shooting started. He thought of the third rider, who had disappeared quickly, and began to hope that Laura Walton had not been made captive.

Hoyt dismounted and untied his medical bag from the cantle of his saddle. He mounted the porch steps and faced the stoop-shouldered woman standing in the shadows.

'Don't worry about Laura, Martha.' Hoyt placed a hand on her shoulder in reassuring fashion. 'She was riding with the Ranger when they ran into trouble on the trail. But Laura can take care of herself.'

The woman turned to Manning, who explained what happened. Hoyt left them and entered the house. There were footsteps in the yard and a man appeared out of the shadows, armed with a rifle.

'Do you plan on staying the night?' the woman enquired. Her face was filled with worry, her eyes showing fear.

'I figure I'll have to, or at least until your daughter shows.' Manning glanced around, worried about the girl. He had known it was wrong to separate despite the shooting. but he had been concerned about her safety. One wild shot could have changed the incident into a nightmare for this family.

'Pete, take care of the horses.' The woman spoke calmly. 'Put them in the barn. Would you like some food?' She looked at Manning pointedly. 'I didn't get your name?'

'Call me Ranger,' he replied. 'I could do with some food, ma'am. How is your husband? Is he badly hurt?'

'I think he'll be all right now Doc is here. Come into the house. Food has been ready some time, but nobody seems to be eating tonight.'

Manning was hungry, and now his investigation had started he had no idea when he might get the chance to eat again. He had learned by hard experience to eat when he could, and he removed his hat and followed the woman into a large kitchen. He ate his fill of the good food available, and by the time he was satisfied he had managed to allay some of the worry in Martha Walton's lined face.

'I can't help wondering what's become of Laura,' the woman said, giving Manning a cup of coffee. 'She ain't one to run from trouble. Did that third man find her in the dark?'

'I'm hoping he didn't, but it sure looks like he did.' Manning shook his head. 'And there's nothing I can do till sunup. When it's light enough to see tracks I'll ride back to where I last saw your daughter and pick up her trail.' He paused, and then added, 'Is there anything you can tell me about the incident your husband suffered?'

'Ben hasn't been conscious long enough to tell me.' Martha shook her head. 'I've been trying for weeks to get him to agree to sell out. We know what's been happening to the other ranchers who were asked to sell. Mort Manning was the last one. He rode over here the day before he was killed and said the situation was getting serious.'

Manning suppressed a sigh, and at that moment Doc Hoyt appeared and came to sit at the table. He glanced at Manning from under shaggy brows.

'Be glad of some food, Martha,' he said.

'What about Ben?' she demanded impatiently.

'I'd have given you any bad news first off.' He grinned. 'There's nothing wrong with Ben that a couple of weeks in bed won't cure. But he's been very lucky. The bullet missed his left lung.' He tossed a misshapen slug of lead on to the table towards Manning, who picked it up. 'If you can find the rifle that fired this bullet you'll have the man responsible.'

'If I could do that I'd have the answers to a lot of the questions bothering me right now.' Manning shook his head. He tucked the bullet into his vest pocket. 'Are you going back to town, Doc?'

'Soon as I've had some food.' Hoyt nodded. 'Mrs Brady is due to have her second child any day now, so I got to stick around town. Is there something I can do for you there?'

'Tell Aitken what happened on the trail. He can arrange to have those two bodies picked up. Come daylight I'm gonna return to the scene and pick up Laura's trail.' He met the doc's gaze as he spoke, and saw the medico tighten his lips. 'I'll spread my bedroll in the barn, if I may,' he said to Mrs Walton. 'I'll be gone before first light, and I'll let you know soon as I can what I find out there.'

The woman thanked him, and Manning left the house and crossed the yard. The guard was standing just inside the barn, and introduced himself as Pete Gannon. He was oldish, dressed in workworn range clothes, and questioned Manning about the shooting.

'Mebbe I better ride with you when you leave,' he said when Manning had recounted the shoot-out with the three unknown riders. 'I know just about everybody in Clearwater County, and if those two dead men ain't complete strangers then I figger I could put a name to them and tell you who they ride for.'

'Thanks for the offer. I reckon you could save me a lot of time. The big question bothering me right now is the identity of those two men I shot, and who their friends are. If I could find out then I reckon I could clean up pronto.' He stifled a yawn. 'But it's no use speculating without facts. I'm gonna hit the sack now. I'll be leaving before first light.'

'I'll be ready and waiting for you,' Gannon told him.

Manning checked his buckskin, gave it some water, then spread his blankets and settled down. His thoughts kept him awake until he managed to clear his mind, and had hardly seemed to fall asleep when Pete Gannon was shaking his shoulder.

'Sun will be up in about an hour,' the old man said hoarsely. 'I figure it will be light enough to read tracks by the time we get to the scene.'

Manning stifled a yawn and got to his feet. He stretched his cramped limbs and quickly prepared for travel. There was one thought in his mind, and that was to locate Laura Walton.

Gannon saddled a bay and they left the ranch quietly, walking their mounts until they were out of earshot. Then they went on quickly, the sound of their hooves echoing in the predawn. The stars were fading in the vast darkness overhead, and already there was faint evidence of greying to the east. The wind was still keen, and was blowing into Manning's face as they continued.

'You reckon it happened on the trail from town, huh?' asked Gannon, 'and about five miles out from the ranch?'

'That's what Laura said when I told her to go on,' Manning retorted.

'I'll tell you when we get to where I figger the spot is. Daylight is coming in fast now.'

Manning looked around, noting that his range of vision was increasing. He felt gaunted, the lack of a good night's sleep filling him with sober reflection. The sudden appearance of the trio of hardcases niggled at his mind, and he was badly worried for the girl's safety.

Full daylight came and Gannon stood up in his stirrups to peer ahead. Manning could see clearly now, and his keen eyes were intently studying the undulating ground. He could see a clear trail in the short grass, and picked out his own hoof-prints, left the night before on his ride to the Tented W with Doc Hoyt. He also saw a single set of prints going back towards town, and figured they had been left by the doc after treating Ben Walton.

'There's a horse standing ahead,' Gannon said suddenly. He had been gazing ahead while Manning kept his gaze on the ground just in front, checking for tracks. He started forward at a canter, but Manning called to him.

'I wanta check the area for tracks before we ride in.'

Gannon reined in, nodding slowly. He dropped back while Manning studied the ground before them, riding at a walk.

There was a horse standing by one of the inert figures lying in the grass, and it whinnied several times as they approached. Manning reined in and looked around while still several feet from the bodies, reading what had happened the night before when the three riders attacked him. He soon spotted the tracks left by Laura Walton when she rode away from him for safety, and turned his horse to follow them. They were widely spaced prints, showing speed and something of the girl's fear.

Manning saw where the third rider had bypassed the fracas, and sighed when he noted the man's tracks converging on those left by the girl. He read the whole grim tale of events from the tracks as plainly as if they had been narrated by an eye-witness, and when he saw two sets of tracks heading due west he nodded to himself. The third rider had come upon the girl in the darkness. She would have called out as he approached, thinking it was Manning himself, and the unknown gunhand had departed with her at his side.

'Got what you wanted?' called Gannon.

'Yeah. The man who left the pair shooting at me picked up Laura and headed due west.' Manning pointed out the two sets of tracks. 'You got any idea what's lying in that direction?'

'Sure. Double M is out that way, about ten miles.'

Manning felt a pang in his chest at the mention of his uncle's spread. He nodded. 'You better take a look at those two I downed and see if you know them,' he suggested. 'I need to know who they were working for. It looks like a human coyote is hiding out on this range, and making a big effort to remain undetected.'

Gannon rode back to where the bodies lay. Dismounting, he took his time checking both corpses, and Manning rolled himself a smoke and sat contemplating until the old cowboy returned to his side.

'I ain't never seen hide nor hair of them two before,' said Gannon. 'They've come from parts unknown. And the horse standing there ain't got a brand on it.'

Manning nodded. 'It's what I expected,' he said grimly. 'It's true that dead men can't talk, but one of the trio is still alive and he's left his tracks for me to follow. I figure you better side me for a spell, Gannon, so you can ride back to Tented W with news, should we gather some.'

'I hope it'll be good news.' Gannon's wrinkled face was set in grim lines. 'I don't like the thought of Miss Laura being at the mercy of saddle scum.'

Manning nodded and sent his horse at a clip to follow the two sets of tracks. He was chafing at the thought that several hours had passed since the girl was taken. But now he had tracks to follow there was a good chance that he would eventually come up with the girl, and he hoped to find her unharmed.

The tracks led on into the west, and eventually joined a well-defined trail meandering from the north.

'This is the main trail to Double M,' said Gannon. 'You're gonna have your work cut out trying to find the killers in this neck of the woods.'

'You figure there's more than one killer?' Manning cuffed back his Stetson and wiped sweat from his rugged forehead.

'It's plain there's a gang behind this trouble,' mused Gannon. 'Some local man has brought in a hard bunch to do his dirty work. There's been several murders, mostly small ranchers, and

Thorpe of Slashed T is the only man able to buy up the spreads of the dead men.'

'Thorpe runs a tough bunch, but that fact alone doesn't make him guilty.' Manning shifted his gaze from the tracks to encompass his surroundings. The prints were plain and easy to follow, and he fought against the impulse to go flat out in pursuit for he had no idea how far he would have to ride.

'Looks like these tracks sure are heading for Double M,' Gannon observed presently. 'Do you figure this hardcase could be holing up there? Mort Manning is dead and the place is deserted except for Hank Tupp and his granddaughter.'

'I heard a man had been put on the ranch as a caretaker,' Manning mused.

'Yeah, and what a choice for a chore like that. Hank Tupp is little better than an out and out badman. He used to run with rustlers, and there was talk a few years back that he had a hand in robbing the bank at Lone Well.'

'Is that a fact?' Manning frowned, his thoughts moving fast. 'In that case I'd better be careful how I ride in.'

He had been looking forward to seeing the ranch his uncle had built up since the end of the civil war, and he certainly intended to find the old man's killer. Initially he had thought the murder of his uncle had been the work of an itinerant badman, but in view of what he was learning about the situation in this county he was now witholding his judgement until he had more facts.

'It's about two miles to Double M now,' Gannon said eventually. 'If you don't want to ride in openly then now's the time to leave the trail. We should cut off the right and sneak into the ranch from the rear.'

'I need to see if these tracks we're following go into the ranch,' Manning said. 'You know this area pretty well, huh?'

'Sure do. I was friendly with Mort

Manning. Used to visit with him often. I'd like to lay my gunsights on the man who killed him. The law wouldn't find much left of him.'

'You got any ideas on who that might be? Did he ever say anything to you when you saw him?'

'Nothing you could work on. Heard him say there were night-riders crossing his range, and he had the usual trouble of fence-cutting and rustling, just like we got at Tented W before Ben Walton was dry-gulched yesterday.'

They continued steadily, until Gannon paused at the foot of a low rise and indicated that the headquarters of Double M were on the other side. Manning checked the ground and saw that the two sets of prints he was trailing skirted the rise and followed its contour around to the right.

'Sure looks like they go smack into Double M's yard,' said Gannon. 'What do you figure on doing?'

'You hole up and watch. I reckon to ride in openly and check the tracks to their end. Then I'll know what to do. Whatever happens, stay out of it. You have to live around here.'

'I'm all for law and order,' Gannon said firmly. 'You get any trouble in there and I'll buy into it.'

Manning departed and skirted the rise, following the trail until he reached the gateway leading into the yard of the ranch. There he paused and looked around more intently. He saw a small wooden ranch house with small windows. There was a pole fence around the yard, a corral to the left, containing six horses, and a barn beyond the corral. Checking the dust of the yard, which was mainly undisturbed, he saw the two sets of tracks he had been following heading straight towards the house.

So Laura Walton had been brought here. Manning studied the tracks. They were hours old. He rode into the yard, still checking the tracks, and saw that they stopped at the house, then continued to the corral. Looking more closely at the horses in the corral, he recognized the one the girl had borrowed from the livery barn in town.

He nodded to himself as he continued to the house, and his eyes narrowed when he saw a squat figure emerge from the building and halt on the porch, feet apart and legs braced, every inch of his heavy body exuding hostility. Manning threw an encompassing glance around the yard, but saw no signs of other men. He returned his attention to the porch, and was now close enough to take in smaller details of the caretaker.

The man was middle-aged, with sun blackened features that were coarse and ugly. His nose was misshapen, had evidently been broken at some time, and his small, beady eyes were filled with bright suspicion and hostility. He looked strong, with hefty arms and thick shoulders, and his right hand, Manning noted, did not stray far from the butt of the sixgun holstered on his right thigh. He wore the gun low, the holster tied down in the manner of a gunman, and as Manning drew nearer he saw the man flick the leather retaining loop off the hammer of the weapon.

'Do somethin' fer you, mister?' The man's voice was harsh, his mouth tight and bad-tempered.

'Are you the boss?' Manning countered.

'There ain't no boss. He's dead. I'm Hank Tupp. I take care of the place. What's it to you?'

'A girl didn't return home last night and I'm helping to look for her.'

'What gal?'

'Laura Walton. She didn't return to Tented W after riding into town yesterday.'

'Is that a fact?' Tupp's heavy shoulders shrugged. 'Well I ain't seen hair or hide of her. Do you think she'd come riding in here to see me?' He laughed hoarsely, and for a moment wicked mirth showed in his dark eyes.'

'You haven't seen her?' Manning

curbed his horse from moving restlessly, holding the animal on a tight rein with his left hand while his right hand lay lightly on his right thigh.

'Ain't I just told you?' Tupp's tone was filled with rising irritation. 'Who in hell are you, mister? I ain't seen you in these parts before.'

'You swear to not seeing the girl?' Manning persisted.

'I ain't in the habit of repeating myself.' The fingers of Tupp's right hand twitched convulsively and moved nearer to the flared gun butt on his right hip.

'But you've seen her horse, huh?'

'Her horse?' Tupp's gaze flickered to the corral and then returned to Manning's ominous figure.

'That's right. Her horse is in your corral. I was with her in town last night when she borrowed that sorrel from the livery barn, and I recognized it when I rode into the yard. Maybe you can tell me how it got here.'

He waited for Tupp's reaction, and

was quite ready for the gunplay that erupted. Tupp made a move for his holstered gun, his right elbow jerking upwards, his clawing fingers grasping his gunbutt, and his sudden movement set Manning flowing into action. Tupp was fast, but Manning drew his Colt and thumbed back the hammer almost before the weapon cleared leather. Tupp had his gun out and was lifting it. But it had not levelled when Manning's trigger finger squeezed hard and sent a chunk of lead smacking into Tupp's right shoulder.

As quick gun echoes shattered the brooding silence, Tupp jerked sideways, his gun exploding harmlessly, sending a bullet into the floor of the porch almost between his own feet. The weapon fell from his suddenly nerveless fingers and he fell back against the wall of the house, his mouth agape, his eyes filled with shock and sudden pain as he slid down to lie on the dusty boards of the porch.

Manning stepped down from his

saddle, gun recocked and ready for further action. His horse skittered away with trailing reins, snorting and blowing nervously, to halt several yards away. Tupp was clasping his right shoulder with his left hand, and, when he tried to push himself upright, he slid sideways until he sprawled on his face to lie groaning in pain.

Manning glanced around quickly, his eyes narrowed, nerves hair-triggered. Gunsmoke rasped in his throat as he drew a quick breath. The harsh echoes of the shooting were fading now, and he covered Tupp mercilessly, determined to get some answers to the questions bothering him.

5

Tupp gazed at Manning with pain-filled eyes, writhing and groaning, blood trickling through the splayed fingers of his left hand pressed against his wound. Manning bent over him, his gun steady and gaping blackly at the centre of Tupp's chest.

'Where's the girl?' Manning demanded.

'She ain't here.' A whimper of pain escaped Tupp.

'I didn't ask you where she ain't.' Manning placed the muzzle of his Colt against Tupp's chin and applied considerable pressure, forcing Tupp's head against the boards of the porch while holding the man's gaze. 'I'm in a hurry, Tupp, and I ain't got time to be pleasant. Answer my question.'

Tupp tried to roll his head sideways to escape the pressure of the gun muzzle. His wound was dripping large splotches of blood. He lay on his back looking up at Manning, his mouth agape and narrowed eyes filled with agony.

'I'm gonna bleed to death,' he gasped hollowly. 'You gotta do somethin' for me.'

'First things first,' Manning growled. 'I got a list of priorities in my mind and you don't figure very high on it.' He glanced around the deserted yard, his eyes narrowed, filled with a bleak expression. 'Where's the girl?'

'Fer Gawd's sake! She's in the house. She was brought in during the night and I was told to keep her here in case she might be needed.'

'Who gave you that order?' Manning grasped Tupp's right elbow and dragged him to his feet. Ignoring his groans, Manning thrust him towards the door of the house, and at that moment he heard the sound of several horses approaching. Throwing a swift glance towards the gate, he saw a trio of riders entering the yard to come at a canter towards the house.

'Who are they?' Manning rasped, thrusting Tupp against the wall of the house and holding him upright with his left hand.

'Trouble for you,' Tupp replied through gritted teeth. 'The one on the right brought the gal in earlier.'

Manning pushed his gun muzzle under Tupp's nose. 'Stand still,' he rapped. 'If you so much as blink I'll kill you!'

'I'm out of it now.' Tupp shook his head. 'I'm bleeding to death.'

The three riders moved apart as they neared the porch, and Manning stood easy, his right hand down at his side, sixgun cocked and ready in his clenched fingers. He could see Tupp out of the corner of his eye, and the man was crouching, groaning softly, but not moving.

'Hold up there,' Manning called. 'Declare yourselves. Who are you and what's your business here?'

'Who in hell are you?' demanded one

of the riders. Dust was puffing up from the hooves of the horses.

'I'm a Texas Ranger. Keep your hands away from your guns and tell me what you are doing here.' Manning's voice echoed across the yard, and he saw the man on the right make a play for his holstered gun, drawing the weapon and lifting it quickly to point it at Manning's big figure.

Tupp immediately uttered a screech of fear and threw himself flat on the dusty boards of the porch. Manning compressed his lips and swung up his right arm, triggering his weapon. Quick gun blasts shattered the silence, and Manning's Colt fired first by a life-saving fraction of a second. His bullet smacked into the chest of the man on the right and sent him plunging over backwards out of his saddle. The nervous horse started away across the yard with the man's foot caught up in the stirrup, and he was dragged through the thick dust.

The other two men were quick to

join the shoot-out and slugs smacked into the front wall of the house close to Manning, who dropped to one knee as a chunk of lead nicked his hatbrim. He swung his Colt, aligning the weapon on the nearest rider, and it bucked against the heel of his hand as he triggered it. Gunsmoke flared, making him blink, and he saw the man spill his gun from suddenly nerveless fingers and fall out of his saddle.

The third man had started to draw his gun, but quickly acknowledged the high standard of Manning's shooting and thrust his weapon deep into its holster. Manning was covering him when the man raised his hands.

Manning drew a deep breath. His eyes were watering. Gunsmoke was hazing thickly along the porch and stinging his nostrils. He stood for a moment, studying the yard. The horse of the first rider had stopped ten yards away, the rider motionless in the dust, his left foot still hooked in a stirrup. The second man had fallen out of his saddle and lay in a crumpled heap, his horse standing with outstretched neck, nuzzling the still figure.

Manning shook his head slowly, then sighed. He glanced at Tupp, who was motionless, flat on his back on the porch, his eyes wide and filled with shock. Then he turned his full attention to the motionless third rider, who was sitting with his hands raised shoulder high. He reloaded the expended chambers of his sixgun and then motioned with the weapon.

'You've proved you've got some sense by surrendering,' he rasped, 'so don't spoil it now. Get rid of your gun and do it slow. Then get down and check your pards. Don't make any sudden moves.'

The man eased his gun from its holster and dropped it into the dust. He turned his horse so that he was in plain view when he dismounted, and stepped down into the yard. Manning watched him checking the two fallen men until his attention was distracted by the sound of the door of the house opening.

He looked round as a woman emerged.

At first glance Manning thought it was Laura Walton, but the newcomer was dark-haired, and older. She looked fearfully across the yard, her hands clasping to her breast at the sight of the fallen men, and then she turned her gaze to Manning, her thin face taut with shock, her eyes wide with fear.

'Where's my grandfather?' she demanded.

'Who would that be?' Manning asked.

'Hank Tupp. He's the caretaker here.'

Manning moved aside so that she could see Tupp, still lying slumped against the front wall of the porch. She uttered a cry and ran to his side.

'Before you touch him go back into the house and turn Laura Walton loose,' Manning ordered.

She looked at him, badly shocked, then expelled her tension in a long, shuddering sigh. 'I told Grandpa he'd find trouble if he mixed with that bad bunch,' she said wailingly. 'But he's so bone-headed he wouldn't listen to me. Did you shoot him or was it one of them?' She threw a contemptuous glance at the figures in the yard.'

'I shot him,' Manning replied.

She nodded and went back into the house. Manning watched the man in the yard. He was coming towards the house now, shaking his head slowly. Manning stood motionless, his gun down at his side again, and the man paused on the bottom porch step.

'They're both dead,' he reported.

'Who are they?' Manning asked.

The man half-turned to look back at the fallen men. 'The one with his foot caught in his stirrup is Butch Wiley. The other is Jack Harmer. Neither of them had any more sense than a dying bullfrog.'

'And who are you?'

'Bill Jones.'

'You're mixed up with this bad bunch.' It was a statement rather than a question, and Manning's hard gaze made the man shrug.

'You got me cold,' he acknowledged. 'I know when I'm beaten, and I ain't fool enough to trade lead with a Ranger.'

'Tell me about Wiley. He was with two men last night who shot at me, and when I downed his pards he kidnapped Laura Walton and brought her here. Who does he work for?'

'Wiley never did a day's work in his life. He runs a gang of rustlers.'

'And you're one of his gang. How come you're using this place as your headquarters?'

'Hank Tupp is running it. He's an old pard. We came to rustle cattle from this spread and saw Tupp. We decided to stay and operate from here. This was the perfect hideout while Tupp was in charge.'

'Yeah, well he's finished as of now, and I'll be taking him and you to jail soon as Tupp can ride. Looks like you've come to the end of your trail, Jones.'

Manning stepped down from the

porch and searched Jones, relieving him of a long-bladed skinning knife that was in a leather sheath suspended between his shoulder blades. Satisfied that Jones no longer posed a threat, he made the man sit down on the edge of the porch with his back to a post and tied his hands behind him around the post with a leather thong which was one of several he had hanging from his belt.

Straightening, he glanced round at the sound of approaching hooves, and saw Pete Gannon coming into the yard. Gannon reined up in front of the porch and dismounted, his face showing shock, his eyes filled with disbelief.

'You handled that trouble so quickly I didn't get the chance to buy into it,' he said.

'There's no trouble now.' Manning smiled grimly. 'And Laura Walton is here. Go on into the house and fetch her out. Then you better take her back to Tented W.'

At that moment Laura Walton emerged from the house and paused in the doorway, followed closely by Tupp's granddaughter. The girl looked tired and shocked, but seemed otherwise unharmed. She came to Manning's side and grasped his hand.

'I'm so glad you've not been hurt,' she said breathlessly. 'When the shooting started last night I thought you'd been killed. Then a man came up to me, and at first I thought it was you. He forced me to go along with him, and I didn't know he'd brought me here until I saw Beth Tupp. They kept me locked in a room.'

'So long as you're not hurt,' Manning said. 'Pete will saddle your horse now and take you home. And you can rest easy about your father. The doc saw him last night and said he'll be all right in a couple of weeks. By the time he's on his feet again the trouble around here will be over. I'll be riding out to talk with your pa when I can find the time.'

Laura thanked him effusively, and Gannon took her across to the corral, where he found her riding gear and prepared to move out. Manning turned his attention to Tupp, whose granddaughter was attending him. He went close.

'Is he hurt too badly to ride?' he demanded.

'Where do you plan on taking him?' she asked.

'To jail, where he belongs. He's been using this place as a roost for rustlers, and that's against the law.'

'I kept telling him he was asking for trouble, mixing with Wiley's bunch.' Beth Tupp shook her head. 'Can't you take pity on him? He's got a good job here, and after this I'm sure he won't get mixed up in anything else.'

'It's not up to me what happens. I only arrest lawbreakers. It's the circuit judge you'll need to appeal to.' He bent over Tupp, who had lapsed into unconsciousness, and looked at the man's wound. 'He'll be able to ride once we've fixed his arm,' he decided. 'You put a bandage on him and I'll take care of the details around here.'

He crossed to the two dead men in the yard and roped them across their saddles, then went back to the house to find that Tupp's wound had been treated. The bleeding had stopped and Tupp was conscious once more, groaning and complaining about his condition.

'I can't sit a saddle,' he protested. 'There's a buckboard over by the barn. I could travel in that.'

'I'll get it ready.' Manning crossed the yard.

Laura Walton was mounted on her horse, and she came across to Manning, still shocked by her experience. But she smiled and thanked him for what he had done. Then she rode out with Gannon, and Manning watched them until they had passed from sight. Then he hitched a team to the buckboard and took it to the house. He tied the horses of the two dead men to the back of the vehicle and handcuffed Jones to a strut inside it.

Tupp complained about being made to travel to town but Manning ignored him, and with the girl driving the buckboard and Manning riding his own horse, they set out for Oaktown.

Evening was drawing on when they reached town, and Manning sighed with relief when they halted in front of the law office. Shadows were crawling into the dusty corners of the street and there were lights showing in some of the windows of the buildings fronting it. Manning stepped down from his saddle and stretched. It had been a long day, but he was well satisfied with what had been accomplished. He threw open the door of the office, and Charlie Aitken sprang up from his seat at the desk, blinking as if he had been aroused from sleep. Manning beckoned him to follow and went out to the sidewalk.

Aitken gaped at the dead men, and Manning left him to jail the prisoners, including Beth Tupp. He sat at the desk and wrote out a report, then faced Aitken, who was lounging near the door leading into the cells. The deputy seemed uneasy, nervously rubbing the law star pinned to his shirt front.

'We've got enough on Tupp and Jones to hold them while I make some more enquiries into their activities on the range,' he said.

'Sure.' Aitken nodded. 'I had the bodies of those two men you killed last night on the trail to Tented W brought in. There'll be an inquest later. What have you got on Tupp?'

'Rustling, I figure. He was allowing a gang of rustlers to stay at Double M. And maybe he knows something about the murders. I figure everything will tie in together. I'm gonna get a bite to eat now. I'll be back to question Tupp.'

'What about the men you killed last night? Doc Hoyt said they shot at you without warning. What was that all about?'

'I got no idea yet,' Manning shook his head. 'But we'll get to the bottom of it.'

'I never set eyes on them before last night,' Aitken said. 'That rustler gang was well hidden out at Double M.'

'Tupp will throw some light on them. I'll question him after the doc has checked his wound.' Manning stood up, drooping with tiredness but aware that his day was far from over. He went to the door then paused and looked back at Aitken. 'I don't know about Beth Tupp yet,' he mused. 'She knew the situation at the ranch. You better hold her for now. And get someone to take care of the bodies outside, and the horses.'

Aitken nodded and Manning left the office and swung into his saddle to ride to the livery barn. Leaving his horse there, he went to an eating house and had his first meal in twenty-four hours, eating in silence, his thoughts mulling over the incidents that had befallen him.

He needed to get proof of the activities of the rustlers Tupp had been hiding. Had they done more than rustle stock? What about the murders that had been committed? He sighed. In his experience, rustlers did not go in for murder. They liked to work as quietly as possible. He nodded, certain that the killings could be linked with a local man. He finished his coffee and got up to leave, and met Sam Askew at the door.

'Howdy.' The lawyer paused, his pale eyes taking in Manning's trail-worn appearance. 'I heard you've been busy on your law work.'

'Have you heard that I shot and arrested Hank Tupp?'

Askew's fleshy face registered shock. 'No! What happened? All I heard was that you killed two men on the trail to Tented W last night.'

'A lot more has happened since then. Let's sit down and I'll give you the details.' Manning returned to the table he had vacated. 'I need to ask you some questions.'

Askew joined him at the table and ordered a meal. When he looked at Manning again his shock at learning of Tupp's arrest had receded. Manning explained what had happened out at Double M and the lawyer listened intently while shaking his head repeatedly in disbelief.

'I asked around before I put Hank Tupp into Double M,' he said at length. 'Tupp seemed reliable and honest, especially with his granddaughter in tow. Now you tell me he's mixed up in the local rustling and might be responsible for the murders. I suppose it's even possible that he killed your uncle at Double M in order to get a foothold for his gang in the county.'

'Once a rustler always a rustler,' Manning observed. 'But Tupp doesn't look like a cold-blooded killer to me.'

'Are you still keeping your real identity secret?' Askew looked into Manning's level gaze. 'Everyone in town is talking about you as the Texas Ranger who's cleaning up around here.'

'I don't need the complication of facing trouble as Mort Manning's nephew come to inherit Double M.' Manning shook his head emphatically.

'That could bring someone like Dallas Thorpe down on my neck, and I don't need a showdown with the likes of Keno Jackson and the tough gunnies who hang around with him. Jackson was ready to tangle with me as the new owner of Double M, but he ain't too keen to mix it with a Texas Ranger.'

'I agree.' Askew nodded. 'I'll hire another caretaker for your ranch.'

'That's what I wanted to talk to you about.' Manning nodded. 'But the next man you put in had better be honest.'

Askew shook his head. 'It was most unfortunate about Tupp. But I assure you that I won't make the same mistake twice.'

Manning got to his feet. 'I'll be talking to Tupp later, and maybe he'll break down and give me full details about the rustling business he's been running. But I've got a feeling I'm being side-tracked by Tupp's activities. I don't think the rustlers are connected with the real trouble that's hit this range.'

'I'm sure you will get to the bottom of it.' Askew nodded. 'You've made a good start.'

Manning took his leave, and stood in the shadows on the street for some minutes, thinking over all that had occurred. He was satisfied with the start he had made, but could not help feeling that somewhere along the line he had missed one or two vital points which had been obscured by the action that had overwhelmed him.

He went along to the saloon to ease his thirst, and found the bar crowded. Standing alone at a corner of the bar, he listened to the many strident voices discussing his exploits, and while he listened his eyes were busy. They narrowed when he spotted Keno Jackson sitting at one of the gambling tables.

He was surprised that the Slashed T foreman could spend so much time away from the ranch. And was he still awaiting the arrival of Mort Manning's nephew? For a moment Manning was tempted to proclaim his identity in order to check Jackson's reaction. If the man tried to kill him it would be a pointer in the right direction. But he decided against such a rash act. He had more important duties to perform before he could turn his attention to personal matters, and it could be that when he solved the murders he might find that his personal problems would vanish with the general lawlessness.

His musing was interrupted by a man who suddenly confronted him. The newcomer was tall and thin, dressed in good range clothes, and seemed to be a cut above the usual run of cowhand. He was in his early fifties, Manning judged, his rugged face trimmed with a fringe of grey beard, his pale eyes open and honest. But he seemed uneasy, and glanced around furtively before speaking.

'You're the Ranger, ain't you?' he asked. 'I'm Rafe Corder. I own the Bar C, which is to the south of Double M. I was in touch with Ranger Headquarters some weeks ago, and I've been waiting for some word from them.'

'Your name was mentioned to me before I left Houston. I'm sorry I haven't had the time to contact you. I've been busy since my arrival.'

'Yeah. And while it's good to see something being done at last, you're being side-tracked.' Corder glanced around, and Manning saw him stiffen when his gaze fell upon the massive figure of Keno Jackson at the gambling table. 'Jackson is one of the men who is running the crookedness in this county. I heard tell you came up against him the minute you reached town. But beating him with your fists won't solve your problems.'

'Have you got proof of Jackson's activities? If you're able to stand up in court and swear to evidence against Jackson then I'll go over now and arrest him.'

'I got the evidence, but I'm not ready to come into the open with it,' Corder replied. 'I'd be dead for sure before the trial started. A lot of men have been scared out of the county or Jackson would have got his come-uppance before now. If you can make this place safe for honest folk then I'll stand up and make some accusations that will stick.'

'Are you prepared to make those accusations without the danger of going public,' Manning asked. 'I'd soon find proof if someone had the nerve to point me in the right direction.'

'Don't count on the reputation of the Rangers protecting you,' Corder warned. 'The minute they thought you posed a threat to them they would have you put away.'

'Thanks for your concern but I don't take anything for granted in this business. What have you got against Jackson?'

'He came out to my place before Mort Manning was killed and asked me if I would sell out. He didn't name a buyer, and I knew he wasn't acting for himself. When I refused to sell he warned me that trouble would come my way.'

'Did he warn you or threaten you?' Manning was looking around the saloon as he spoke and saw that Jackson was watching Corder and himself. He saw the Slashed T ramrod speak to one of his two sidekicks, and the man arose from the gaming table and went quickly to the batwings to disappear into the night.

'He put it as a warning.' Corder laughed harshly. 'But he was threatening at the same time. After that I began to be troubled by night riders and rustling. There was some fence cutting, and some of the gunnies that Jackson ramrods began to go on the prod whenever me or my family came to town. It got so bad that we don't come into Oaktown any more. But I heard you were here and I had to risk seeing you.'

'I'll put Jackson in jail and then come back to you,' suggested Manning.

'You'd have to put the whole bunch

of them behind bars before I would dare open my mouth.' Corder grimaced. 'And if this has happened to me then you can bet it's happened to others around here. Why don't you ask around?'

'Yeah.' Manning nodded, recalling that Martha Walton had said her husband contacted Ranger Headquarters in the hope of getting help. 'I'll get around to it soon as I can, Corder. I figure if I can get all the smaller ranchers to band together in their complaints then we'll have a better chance of beating these criminals.'

A gun crashed as Corder opened his mouth to agree, and the man stiffened, his eyes widening. He fell forward against Manning, blood spurting from his mouth. Manning instinctively caught the sagging body. He looked around and saw a plume of gunsmoke belching in over the batwings, and when he glanced in Jackson's direction he saw a grin on the big man's fleshy face.

6

For a split second Manning was shocked motionless, then he lowered Corder's body to the sawdust and ran to the batwings, where the cloud of blue gunsmoke was drifting lazily into the long room. His action broke the spell that gripped everyone present, and men moved again and began converging on the spot where the dead man lay.

Manning reached the batwings and shouldered his way out to the sidewalk. The night was dark, and the lanterns burning at intervals along the street were not much help to his vision. But he saw a tall figure running away to the right along the sidewalk and gave immediate chase. A man brushed his left elbow in passing, and Manning reached out and grasped his arm.

'Did you see the guy who fired a shot into the saloon?' he demanded.

The man's face was a pale blur in the shadows. He jerked his arm free of Manning's grip. 'I didn't see nothin',' he said hoarsely, and hurried on his way, bootheels hammering rapidly on the board-walk.

Manning saw the running man duck into an alley and disappear. He gave chase, checking his surroundings with narrowed gaze. There were other figures along the sidewalk, but no one seemed to be in a hurry. He reached the alley where the running man had disappeared. Impenetrable darkness filled its length, but at that moment a door opened almost at the far end of the alley and a shaft of yellow lamplight briefly illuminated the area. Then a door banged, abruptly cutting off the light, and Manning hurried into the darkness, easing his gun in its holster. His left hand was outstretched, fingers in contact with the wall at his side, and he widened his eyes in order to catch as much light as possible. He saw a faint glow ahead, which turned out to be a masked lantern over a doorway. When he reached the doorway he paused to check his surroundings.

The sound of a piano playing faintly reached his ears and he fumbled for a door handle. Finding one, he opened the door and light flared out around him while the music rose in volume. He entered a small anteroom where a large, well dressed woman was seated at a desk by an inner door. She was well past middle age, her wrinkled face heavily made up. She looked up at Manning, and a shadow crossed her face as she studied him.

'A man came in here within the last few moments,' Manning rapped. 'Where did he go?'

'There ain't been anyone in here in the last hour.' There was hostility in the woman's tone.

'You're lying. I saw him enter. If you cover for him you're obstructing the law and laying yourself open to charges.'

'Are you a lawman?' The woman's face turned pale under its coating of powder and rouge.

'I'm a Texas Ranger. You better change your story or I'll put you behind bars.'

'Mack Jenson ducked in here a few minutes ago. He went on through.' The woman jerked a thumb at the inner door. 'Said he wasn't staying but taking a short cut to the livery barn. What did he do?'

'Who is Mack Jenson?'

'One of the two gunnies who shadows Keno Jackson whenever he's in town.'

'And what's your name?' Manning was recalling the features of the two men he had seen with Jackson and remembered the man who had left the saloon on Jackson's orders just before the shooting.

'Every man in town knows me by sight.'

'I don't, so tell me who you are and I'll know you the next time I see you.'

'I'm Sal Martin.'

'I'll remember that.' Manning turned

and went back out to the alley. He hurried to the back lots and turned right to make for the stable.

Reaching the livery barn Manning slid in against the back wall and eased sideways until he came to the wide rear doorway. There was lantern light inside, and he wrinkled his nose at the sharp horse smell emanating from the stalls. A tall figure was standing at the street end of the stable, and Manning watched it intently as he went forward silently, checking each stall as he passed it.

About halfway along the stable a faint movement in a stall on his left caught his eye and he instinctively side-stepped as he turned to face it. As quick as he was he was almost too late, for the prongs of a hayfork barely slid by his chest.

Manning caught his breath, it had been so close. He lifted his hands to grapple with the big, shapeless figure wielding the fork and shifted his weight quickly to his left foot. He kicked with his right boot and made contact with the man's body.

The jolt of the contact threw him sideways off balance, and he crashed against a wooden partition, twisting as he did so to keep his assailant in view. The man had taken Manning's kick on the thigh instead of the belly, and was trying to jerk the prongs of the fork free of the stall, where his initial lunge had embedded them. When it wouldn't budge he let go of it and turned to face Manning, his right hand dropping to the butt of his holstered gun.

Manning slid his left foot forward, and as the man's sixgun cleared leather he kicked again, the toe of his right boot connecting with the man's gun-hand. The weapon flew from the man's grasp. Manning followed up swiftly, his left fist swinging in a tight arc. His knuckles smacked meatily against the side of the man's jaw. The man staggered backwards, arms flailing the air, and Manning's right fist hit him on the other side of the jaw and sent him inertly to the ground.

A gun blasted and a bullet plucked the shirt at Manning's left shoulder from behind, branding his flesh with streaking pain. The crash of the shot was deafening in the close confines of the stable as Manning dropped instantly, his right hand clawing for the flaring butt of his holstered gun. He hit the ground on his back and rolled to face the new menace. There was a man standing in the next stall, poking the muzzle of a sixgun through a hole in the woodwork and drawing a fresh bead on Manning.

Manning lifted his Colt, and when the foresight covered the man's chest he squeezed the trigger. The weapon bucked powerfully in his hand, erupting in flame and smoke. The bullet took the man in the centre of the chest and he went down out of sight as if he had been swatted by a giant hand.

Manning's ears were protesting at the noise. He pushed himself to his feet and backed into a corner, ready for anything. But the echoes died away and an uneasy silence slowly returned. He looked at the man unconscious at his feet, then checked his surroundings cautiously. For the moment he seemed to be alone, and he went quickly into the next stall and bent to examine the man who had shot at him. He found the man sprawled dead, and made a conscious effort to ease his tension.

The figure that had been standing in the front doorway of the barn when Manning entered from the rear had ducked outside when the shooting started. Now, hearing Manning's movements, he came cautiously back into the doorway. The lantern hanging in the doorway threw a yellow glare over Manning, and the man paused.

'You're the Ranger,' he gasped.

'Yeah. Did you know there were men laying for me?'

'Did I hell!' The stableman sounded indignant. 'I don't allow trouble in my barn'

'One of them is dead. Come and take

a look at them. I need to know who they are.'

They returned to the stall, and the man Manning had stunned was beginning to stir.

'Heck, that's Al Spence. He rides for Slashed T. He came into town about half an hour ago. The ostler went into the next stall and bent over the dead man. He looked up at Manning, his face shadowed.

'This is Will Bennett. He rides for Ben Walton.'

'Is that Ben Walton of Tented W?'

'None other, and Walton was dry-gulched a couple of days ago. Now why is one of his crew siding someone attacking a Ranger?'

'The questions can wait,' Manning cut in. 'Hogtie Spence and I'll have him picked up and taken to the jail. I came in here looking for Mack Jenson. Where is he?'

'Jenson! Another Slashed T gunnie! You just missed him. He came in through the rear door two minutes ahead of you.' The stableman paused. 'Say, that's strange. Jenson has been in town for days with Jackson. His horse was unsaddled. But when he came in he grabbed the horse, ready-saddled, and high-tailed it out of here. I guess Spence must have saddled up for him. They must have been expecting trouble. When Jenson went out with his horse I thought he was in a hurry to get back to the ranch but he went along the street. He's most likely gone for a drink before riding back to Slashed T.'

'What colour shirt is Jenson wearing?' Manning asked.

'Shirt?' The stableman was surprised. 'Er, I reckon it was pale green. But I couldn't swear to that.'

Manning nodded and went along the street towards the saloon. He was cold inside, his mind searching for answers to the questions bothering him. But he did not relax his alertness. There was a horse tethered to the hitching rail in front of the saloon and he checked out the animal, finding a Slashed T brand on its left rump. He mounted the steps to the sidewalk and peered into the saloon. Keno Jackson was standing at the bar, and his two regular sidekicks were with him.

The gunnie wearing the green shirt, Jenson, was on Jackson's left. Tall and thin, his face was loutish, fleshy and fierce-expressioned, but Manning noted that he was on edge, his gaze flickering around the saloon. He was the man Jackson had sent out of the saloon just before the shot was fired that killed Corder. Shifting his gaze, Manning saw Rafe Corder stretched out in the sawdust with Doc Hoyt bent over him. Charlie Aitken and several men were standing nearby, watching the doc's ministrations.

Manning pushed through the batwings and walked to the bar. He saw Jackson glance his way and then turn his head quickly to speak to Jenson. Manning did not break his stride. He passed Jackson and drew level with Jenson, then spun swiftly and stepped in behind Jenson, reaching for the man's holstered sixgun and lifting it. The three clicks as he cocked the weapon sounded unnaturally loud in the tense atmosphere.

'What the hell!' Jenson slapped his hand to his empty holster.

'Take it easy,' Manning said. 'Your gun killed Corder. Stand still, unless you want to be the second victim in here. You're under arrest for murder.'

Jackson opened his mouth to protest then thought better of it. Manning backed off a step, tilting Jenson's gun and sniffing the muzzle.

'This gun has been fired recently,' he observed.

'I shot at a rattler on my way to town,' Jenson growled. 'I just rode in from the ranch. My hoss is hitched to the rail outside. When I walked in here, Corder was already dead.'

'You were in here with Jackson when I came in,' Manning corrected. 'When Corder spoke to me, Jackson sent you outside, and a moment later a shot was fired which killed Corder. I figure you reckoned his mouth had to be closed. You're lying, Jenson, and I'm taking you for murder.'

Manning heard boots thudding on the boards at his back and threw a quick glance over his shoulder. Doc Hoyt was coming towards him, his lined face harshly set, and Charlie Aitken was following behind the medico like a pet dog, frowning and looking generally uneasy.

'Rafe Corder is dead.' The doc spoke as if his words burned his mouth. 'You got the deadwood on this galoot?'

'I reckon.' Manning broke Jenson's sixgun and examined the loads. One shell was empty and Manning removed it from the weapon and dropped it into his pocket.

'I tell you I fired that shot at a rattler on my way into town,' Jenson snarled.

'Dig out the bullet that killed Corder and let me have it, Doc,' Manning said. 'I'll be able to tell if Jenson's gun fired it.'

'Soon as I can, and with great pleasure,' Hoyt replied.

Manning glanced at Aitken. 'Take Jenson to the jail and lock him in a cell,' he ordered.

Jackson began to protest, and Manning stuck the muzzle of the gun he was holding into the big ramrod's side.

'Forget it for now,' he rasped, and lifted Jackson's weapons from his holsters and dropped them to the floor. 'I don't doubt that Jenson was acting on your orders, so we'll all go to the jail and try to sort it out. I got some questions to ask you, Jackson, and I'll be interested in your answers.' He looked at the third Slashed T gunman, who was standing motionless and silent, and waggled the gun in his hand. 'You better come along too,' he said. 'Shuck your gunbelt and tell me your name.'

'I'm Cal Evans,' the gunnie said, unbuckling his gunbelt and letting it fall to the floor. 'I ain't mixed up in this.'

Jackson began to protest angrily and

Manning jabbed him with the muzzle of his gun.

'Not now,' Manning shook his head. 'I got more than enough evidence to hold you, Jackson. There's a dead man down at the livery barn, and another Slashed T gunnie is a prisoner there — Al Spence, who will shortly be in jail. They ambushed me after you passed through the barn, Jenson, and that is gonna take a lot of explaining.'

Jackson looked into Manning's eyes, saw the deadly intention there, and shrugged. Manning backed off, gun steady. He saw that Aitken had drawn his gun and was covering the Slashed T trio, but there was reluctance showing on the deputy's face. Aitken looked as if he wished it were Manning under arrest.

The prisoners were taken to the jail and locked in cells, all protesting their innocence and demanding to be freed. Manning sent Aitken along to the livery barn to bring in Spence, and sat down to consider the implications of what had occurred. When he had sorted out the questions that needed to be asked and answered he arose, picked up the cell keys and went into the cell block prepared for a hassle with the prisoners.

Keno Jackson was talking furiously to Jenson, but he fell silent when Manning appeared. Manning went to the cell where Jenson was sitting alone and unlocked the door.

'Into the office,' he said. 'You've been telling him what to say, huh, Jackson?'

'We don't know a thing about Corder getting killed,' Jackson snarled. 'You're making a big mistake, Ranger. Jenson didn't ride into town until after the shot was fired, so it couldn't have been him.'

'I saw Jenson with you when I entered the saloon before Corder showed up,' Manning replied. 'I guess I've got the rights of it.'

Jenson emerged from the cell and started into the office. Manning had not drawn his gun, and suddenly Jenson whirled and sprang at him. Manning had been expecting an attack, and his right fist flashed out in a wicked arc, his hard, raw-boned knuckles smacking flush against the prisoner's jaw. Jenson went down like a pole-axed steer. Manning rubbed his knuckles. He grasped Jenson's shirt front, lifted him bodily and dragged him into the office.

Jenson groaned and his eyes flickered when Manning dumped him in a chair. Manning moved back a couple of paces and waited for the prisoner to recover his senses. Jenson's head lolled, and Manning slapped him lightly across the face.

'Come on, wake up,' he snapped.

Jenson lifted his head. His eyes were open, and Manning saw a glint in their dark depths and was not lulled into a sense of false security. He pulled forward a chair and sat astride it, arms resting on the high back. Jenson pushed himself erect, and there was a sneer on his unshaven face.

'I know your story,' said Manning. 'You rode into town from Slashed T, arriving after Corder had been killed.

You account for your gun having been fired recently by claiming that you shot a snake on your way into town.'

'That's right, so you can turn me loose.'

'You know what's wrong with your yarn. I noticed you in the saloon when I arrived, and after Corder was shot I saw you running away from the saloon. You ducked into the first alley on the right, and I followed you.'

'It's dark out on the street. You couldn't have seen anyone.'

'I followed you into the alley, and you went into the local cat-house. I was just behind you. I spoke to Sal Martin at the desk in there and she identified you, told me you went straight through and out the back door, heading for the stable. She named you all right.'

'That's a lie.'

'It'll be your word against hers and mine.' Manning smiled. 'And I figure I know who the judge will believe. But that's not the end of it. When I got to the stable I was jumped by Spence and

Bennett. I was forced to kill Bennett, but Spence is under arrest. Also, the stableman saw you collect your horse and go along the street to the saloon. That makes a real mess of your statement, huh? You better do some serious thinking, Jenson, and then try to come up with the truth. It might help your case if you come clean.'

The street door opened and Al Spence entered, followed by Aitken. Spence's hands were tied behind his back. He looked to be still dazed from tangling with Manning.

'Put Jenson back in his cell,' Manning told Aitken. 'He's guilty of murder.'

'Did he admit to that?' Aitken demanded.

'He doesn't have to.' Manning gazed at Jenson, who was now looking discomfited. 'I got the dead-wood on him.'

Aitken drew his gun to escort Jenson into the cell block. Manning untied Spence's hands and motioned for him to sit down. The hardcase obeyed, gazing at Manning with unblinking eyes.

'What were you doing in the stable with Bennett, and why did you attack me?' Manning asked.

'We thought you were someone else.' Spence was a big man, beefy, with muscular arms and large hands.

'Who?'

'That ain't none of your business.'

'You know me by sight, and you came at me from behind with a hayfork. If I hadn't side-stepped I would have been skewered. If it wasn't me you were after then who was it and why did you want to kill him?' He paused for a reply but Spence sat gazing mutely at him. 'You were at the stable to prevent anyone following Jenson when he made his escape after killing Corder. You're in bad trouble, Spence, and you'll go to prison for a long time if you don't level with me.'

Spence shook his head, and Manning tried another angle.

'You ride for Slashed T, huh?'

'So?'

'What's going on around here? Men are being dry-gulched and killed. And I've just put three other Slashed T crew behind bars. What's with you guys?'

'You got three of the crew in here?' Surprise edged Spence's voice. 'Who are they?'

'Keno Jackson, Jenson and Evans. Jenson is going to be charged with Corder's murder. Now tell me what went on in town today.'

'I got nothing to say. I ain't mixed up in murder, and you can't prove I was.'

Manning shook his head. 'OK,' he decided. 'If you ain't gonna tell the truth then I'll leave you to sweat for a spell. On your feet. You know where the cells are.'

Spence got to his feet and Manning escorted him into the cell block. Jenson had been locked in his cell and Aitken was talking to Jackson.

'Get Hank Tupp and bring him into the office,' Manning ordered, and

Aitken went along the passage to the cells at the far end of the block. 'And bring his granddaughter too.'

He locked Spence in an empty cell and waited for Tupp to reach him. The old man was nursing his shoulder wound, grunting at the effort of walking. He looked enquiringly into Manning's face as he went into the office, and Manning glanced back and saw Beth Tupp emerging from her cell. He waited for her to reach him.

'How long are you going to keep me locked up?' the girl demanded.

'Until I can get the straight of what's been going on at Double M.' Manning escorted her into the office. Hank Tupp was already slumped in a seat, his face grey with shock. The girl went to her grandfather's side and sat with him, holding his hand.

Manning sat on a corner of the desk. He heard Aitken lock the door to the cell block. The deputy dropped the cell keys on the desk and went on to the street door.

'I got to make a round of the town,' he said. 'I don't figure you need me here.'

Manning nodded and Aitken departed. Manning considered for a moment, then turned his attention to Tupp.

'So what was going on out at Double M?' he asked.

'I couldn't do anything about the situation out there,' Tupp replied heavily. 'A bunch of rustlers took over the place. I had to do what they told me or they might have harmed Beth. I was real glad when you showed up, Ranger. They were getting nasty.'

'You were so glad to see me you tried to pull a gun on me,' Manning said harshly. 'You knew those rustlers. You worked with them at one time. You were at Double M as the caretaker, and you brought in that gang of rustlers to clean out the range.'

'That ain't true,' Tupp whined.

'Why was Laura Walton kidnapped?'

'I don't know. Wiley showed up with her and told me to keep her under cover for a spell.'

Manning looked at Beth Tupp. 'Is there anything you want to add to what your grandfather says?' he asked.

'I don't know anything about it,' she replied. 'I was scared of those hardcases hanging around the ranch, and now we're homeless.'

'Pity you didn't think about that before getting mixed up in this business,' Manning retorted.

'You better let Sam Askew know no one is out at Double M right now,' Tupp said uneasily. 'Someone should be on the spread or those rustlers will pull it apart stick by stick.'

'How many rustlers are there? I killed four.'

'There's a dozen of them.' Tupp spoke reluctantly.

'Are they working with local men?' Manning waited for a reply and saw Tupp glance at his granddaughter and shake his head. The girl had opened her mouth to speak, but at Tupp's signal she firmed her lips and looked down at the floor. 'You could be in a lot of trouble,' Manning told her. 'Up to now I ain't got much against you, Miss Tupp, so if you help me with my enquiries it could help at your trial, if I decide you have to be charged.'

'You're bluffing,' Tupp rasped. 'We both know you don't have anything against Beth. You ain't got nothin' on me, come to that. When I tried to draw on you I didn't know you was a Ranger. I was just trying to do my job protecting Double M.'

'I'd give you the benefit of the doubt if I got some real help in finishing this crooked business,' Manning offered. 'Think it over. I'll talk to you again in the morning. I want to know who's behind the dry-gulching and murdering. Who killed Mort Manning? Was it Slashed T? I've got Jenson for killing Rafe Corder. Spence rides for Slashed T. Is Dallas Thorpe running this crooked business?'

Tupp shook his head and Manning suppressed his impatience and got to his feet. He picked up the cell keys, returned Beth and Henry Tupp to their cells and locked them in. On his way back to the office he halted at Jackson's cell and peered in at the Slashed T ramrod. Jackson glowered at him, the bruises on his heavy face dull and angry-looking.

'Why did you have Rafe Corder killed?' Manning asked.

'Me? You got to be kidding. Why would I want him dead? I got no axe to grind.'

'Were you afraid that he'd talk to me, pass on something that would incriminate either you or your boss?'

'You're clutching at straws, Ranger.'

'I managed to have a chat with Corder before Spence killed him. He told me you visited his ranch and made an offer to buy the spread but you didn't say who wanted it. I figure you made the offer on another's behalf. Who was it?'

'I don't know what you're talking about.'

Manning nodded and turned away. 'You'll have plenty of time to think things over,' he promised. 'We'll get to the bottom of it in time.'

He returned to the office to find a small, middle-aged man standing by the desk, checking a double-barrel shotgun.

'Who are you?' Manning demanded.

'Night jailer. Name of Frank Miles. You must be the Ranger. Sure is a lot of talk about you round town tonight. There ain't been so much activity since the Alamo. You just about finished the crooked business, huh?'

Manning shook his head. 'It's a long way from finished. But I got high hopes. You've got a jail full of prisoners tonight. Can you handle it?'

'Sure thing. They'll still be here come morning.' Miles loaded his shotgun, closed it, then laid it on the desk near to his hand. 'If you're on your way out I'll lock the street door behind you,' he added pointedly.

'I guess I done enough for one day.' Manning stifled a yawn. 'It's time I got some sleep. See you in the morning, Miles.'

He left the office and stood for a moment on the sidewalk. Miles closed and bolted the door, and Manning heaved a sigh and tried to relax. He felt the need of another beer before turning in for the night, and headed back the saloon. He was still pounding the sidewalk when a spate of shots blasted out the silence at the far end of town and gun flashes split the darkness.

Manning clenched his teeth and started running towards the disturbance. There were at least six guns being fired and he wondered what the disturbance meant. Had the man bossing the crooked deal around here decided to come out into the open? He drew his gun as he ran, ready for anything, although there was a tiny voice in the back of his mind warning him to beware of ambush.

7

Manning was halfway along the street when six shadowy riders came at a gallop down the centre of it, whooping and firing their sixguns into the air. The town echoed and re-echoed to the quick gun blasts, and Manning frowned and eased his gun in its holster. He paused beside a post and watched the riders. They were heading for the jail end of town, and he wondered if they were about to hit the law office. But they wheeled their mounts at the end of the street and came back yelling and firing into the air like a party of raiding Indians.

A lone rider was coming along the street and the six hell-raisers split and passed him, to continue to the stable end of town. Manning stepped down into the dust and moved out to the centre of the street to confront the rider. A moment later the man reined up in front of him. Manning was angered when he recognized Dallas Thorpe, and the Slashed T rancher lifted a hand to his hat in mock salute.

'Howdy, Ranger.' Thorpe's face was shadowed from the dim street lanterns by the wide brim of his Stetson. 'You're just the man I wanta see.'

The riders were coming back along the street. The shooting had ceased and the echoes were fading slowly, rolling away out of town. The six gunslingers slowed from the gallop and rode in behind Thorpe, reining up to sit motionless at the back of their boss. All guns were holstered now. Dust settled slowly, and Manning was keenly aware of the silence that closed in about them. He was aware, too, of townsfolk emerging cautiously from cover to line the sidewalks, attracted by the spate of shooting.

'What's the idea of disturbing the peace?' Manning asked. He was wondering where Charlie Aitken had gotten to, for there was no sign of the deputy, who should have been the first man on the scene. 'You know I could throw the whole bunch of you in jail for firing guns in a public place and disturbing the peace.'

'Heck, we came into town to offer the law our services.' Thorpe grinned, his teeth gleaming in the night. 'I heard about the trouble you had out at Tented W and Double M, and as you've got just one no-account deputy sheriff to rely on I figured to back the law and give it some real muscle.'

'The law is not in need of help, and I could soon raise a posse if I needed assistance. Disperse your men, Thorpe, and if this happens again the whole bunch of you will see the inside of the jail.'

'You're making a big mistake, Ranger.' Thorpe shook his head. 'But if that's the way you want it then who am I to argue? You heard the man, boys. Go get yourselves a drink before we head back to the ranch.'

The riders wheeled their mounts and rode to the saloon, whooping and raising dust. Thorpe sat facing Manning, and for a moment they gazed impassively at one another. Manning was tempted to jail the Slashed T boss for the night, but he was not ready to force a showdown. He needed more evidence to back his play successfully. Thorpe laughed, apparently well aware of the problems facing the law. He raised a hand to his hat and began to wheel his mount away.

'Hold it,' Manning snapped. 'I need to talk to you.'

'Sure. What's on your mind?' Thorpe stepped down from the saddle and led his horse to the nearest hitching rail.

Manning explained the events that had occurred in town, and Thorpe listened without interruption. When Manning lapsed into silence the big rancher shook his head and whistled softly through his teeth.

'That don't sound too good,' he remarked. 'So you figure Mack Jenson murdered Rafe Corder, and on Jackson's orders.'

'I got the deadwood on Jenson.'

'And Spence and Bennett laid for you! That don't make sense. Why would they want to kill a Ranger? I guess everyone knows that when a Ranger is killed the Rangers never rest till they get the killer. And I've always insisted that my crew, whoever they are, should respect the law at all times.'

'I was hoping you could shed some light on this business,' Manning said softly.

'Me? How would I know what's going on?'

'Let's try and find out. Jackson and two gunslingers are in town waiting for Manning to turn up. They can only be here on your orders, and I'd like to know how you instructed Jackson.'

Thorpe sighed. 'I know all about the trouble in this county,' he said thickly. 'Mort Manning was murdered, and there's been a lot of conflict. As one of the biggest ranchers on the range I figure I owe it to the community to back the law. That's why those three men are in town. I was afraid that when Manning arrived he would be gunned down like his uncle was. Jackson was ordered to watch out for Manning and bring him to see me soon as he arrived. I planned to protect him until he had settled in and hired his own crew.'

'Jackson wasn't following those instructions. When I first rode in he figured I was Manning, and was ready to pull his gun on me. But apart from that, you're the only man making a profit from these smaller ranchers being scared out. You've bought out several at prices so low they're practically robbery.'

'I'm the only man around here with enough ready cash to pay the people who want to get out quick, and I'm in business to make a profit.'

'So you're making a fat profit from other men's misery.'

'There's no law against that! If I didn't buy them out they would still be here, and probably dead by now.'

'So who in this county is causing all the trouble just so you can make a profit?'

'Are you accusing me?'

'Not right now. These are questions I have to ask, and if I don't get satisfactory answers I'll want to know why. Can you think of anyone around here who would frighten the smaller ranchers so you can buy them out?'

Thorpe shook his head. 'There are two sides to that question. You're looking at it from your point of view, but I see it as some unknown person taking advantage of the fact that I am buying out the unfortunates. Someone is making it look like I am guilty of what you suspect.'

Manning nodded. He had half-expected that answer. 'So why did Keno Jackson and his two hardcases act like they did? Jenson is gonna be charged with murder. Do you expect me to believe they deliberately went against your orders? Jenson shot Corder in cold blood, and Corder is yet another small rancher. He told me before he was shot that Jackson had offered to buy him out and when he refused to sell he began to get trouble. Were you planning to buy Corder out?'

'I asked him to sell when I heard he was thinking of pulling his stakes but he refused.' Thorpe shrugged. 'I guess that looks bad, huh?'

'That's right, and there are more questions I'd like to ask, but I don't figure I'll get the right answers yet. I reckon we can straighten out some of this though. Come along to the jail and let's ask Jackson why he disobeyed your orders?'

'Are you charging him with any crime?'

'I don't know until I've had a chance to check up.'

Thorpe turned away. 'I'll head back to the ranch now.'

'And don't bring your crew back into town yelling and shooting,' Manning said. 'There'll be hell to pay if you do.'

Thorpe chuckled and led his horse away. Manning stood in the shadows, looking around. The townsfolk had drifted away and he was alone. Charlie Aitken still had not put in an appearance, and Manning decided to look for the deputy.

Thorpe was calling his crew out of the saloon when Manning reached it, and the tough gunnies grinned as they filed past Manning, who stood at the batwings. When they had gone, the sound of their hooves fading along the street, Manning went to the bar and bought a beer.

'You seen anything of Aitken?' he asked when the tender slid a foaming glass before him.

'Not since he left to pick up Spence at the stable.'

Manning took his beer into a corner where he could watch the scene and not be a part of it. His thoughts were busy, and for a time they were concentrated on Charlie Aitken. Then he finished his beer and went out to the sidewalk. He walked towards the jail, aware that he could not postpone the things that should not be be delayed.

The front windows of the law office were bright with lamplight, and, as he approached, Manning recalled the day of his arrival. He had been shot at from the far corner of the jail, and at that time only two men in town had been aware that he was Chuck Manning — one being Askew the lawyer, and the other Shreeve, the banker. So why had he been shot at? Keno Jackson had been the only man who had shown any animosity, but he had not been prepared to act without proof of Manning's identity. Had either Askew or Shreeve passed on the vital information?

He opened the door of the office and crossed the threshold, then paused, for the night jailer was lying on the floor beside the desk and there was blood on his head. Manning drew his gun, noting that the door to the cell block was ajar, and the big bunch of cell keys was not on the desk.

Manning cocked his gun and cat-footed across the office, pulling the door to the cells wide open. A lighted lantern was hanging from a nail about halfway along the passage, throwing a pool of soft light around the centre of the passage but leaving the far end in shadow. Manning squinted his eyes to pierce the gloom at the farther end. A strong draught was blowing into his face and he saw a figure at the heavy wooden back door, which was open.

'What in hell is going on?' Manning called. He glanced around and saw that the nearer cells, which had contained Jackson and the other Slashed T men, were empty, their doors standing wide open.

The figure at the back door swung round, and Manning sensed rather than saw the swift elbow movement as the man made a play for his holstered gun. He was already covering the figure, and lifted his thumb from his gun hammer. The weapon blasted, filling the jail with raucous sound, and Manning gritted his teeth as acrid gunsmoke enveloped him. He saw the figure jerk, then pitch to the ground, and went forward swiftly.

He was not unduly surprised to see that it was Charlie Aitken lying in a heap beside the door, a splotch of blood on his shirt front. Manning bent over the deputy and discovered that he was alive, and straightened to check the cells. Hank and Beth Tupp were still locked up, but the rustlers who had been at Double M were also gone with the Slashed T men.

'What happened here?' Manning demanded.

'That skunk Aitken showed his true colours at last,' said Beth Tupp. 'He turned your prisoners loose and let them out the back door. I heard horses out back before Aitken came in.'

So that was why the deputy had not put in an appearance when the Slashed T riders were hurrahing the town. Thorpe had caused a diversion while Aitken turned the prisoners loose.

Manning clenched his teeth. He went back to Aitken and checked the man again. The deputy was unconscious, breathing shallowly, and, collecting Aitken's gun, Manning checked the back door was locked and took the keys into the office.

The night jailer was beginning to stir, and Manning propped him in a chair.

'What happened?' Miles demanded between groans, holding his head in both hands.

'I was hoping you could tell me,' Manning rapped. He was furious that so much good work had been wasted.

'Aitken came in and stood beside me at the desk, and that's all I can remember. He must have slugged me, the dirty skunk. Where is he?'

'In the cell block with a bullet in his chest.' Manning half turned to face the street door as it was thrust open, and he was pleased to see Doc Hoyt entering. 'You're always one of the first on the scene when there's been a shooting,' he observed.

'It's a habit I've cultivated over the years,' Hoyt said. He bent over the night jailer and examined his head. 'You better go home and take it easy for a day or so,' he advised. He glanced at Manning. 'What was that shot I heard?'

'Aitken is lying in the cell block shot in the chest. I think he's far gone.' Manning opened the door leading into the cells and the doctor hurried past him. Manning remained in the doorway and watched the doc. Hoyt knelt beside the stricken deputy, and almost immediately got to his feet and came back to where Manning was standing.

'He's dead,' he remarked. 'How did it happen?'

Manning explained, and Hoyt shook his head.

'I never did cotton to Aitken,' he said. 'There was always something about him that was not right.'

'I got the same feeling when I met him,' Manning agreed. 'Look, I got a lot to do, Doc. I need to get the prisoners back, and there's still a lot of evidence I need to collect.'

'Sure. You do what you have to.'

Manning checked his gun as he walked across the office, and reloaded the empty chamber. He went out into the night and pushed through the gathering townsmen, who had been attracted by the shot. Ignoring them, he hurried along the sidewalk to the livery barn, and found the stableman in his office.

'Howdy.' The man got to his feet. 'Are you going to San Lorenzo as well?'

'San Lorenzo?' Manning frowned.

'Yeah.' The stableman nodded. 'Aitken was in here earlier. Said all the prisoners were being taken to the county seat. He saddled half a dozen mounts and led them along the street. And he was in a real hurry. I never saw him move so fast.'

'That's all I want to know.' Manning turned away.

He went back to the jail, where the crowd was still waiting for news. The undertaker emerged from the office followed by two men who had Aitken's covered body on a stretcher. Doc Hoyt emerged and departed quickly. Manning went into the office. The night jailer was sitting at the desk, his head in his hands. He looked up at Manning, then got to his feet, groaning softly and rubbing his head.

'Are you staying on duty?' Manning demanded.

'There ain't anyone else to take over,'

'I will. I'll sleep in here tonight.' Manning was angry at the way Thorpe had deceived him. 'You better go home and rest up. I'll need you on duty tomorrow morning.'

'I'll be back in the morning.' The jailer made for the door and departed.

Manning bolted the street door. He went through to the cell block, picked up the lantern, and unlocked the back door. Careful not to obliterate any tracks, he held the lantern aloft and studied the ground outside. The prints of half a dozen horses were quite plain in the thick dust. He closed the door again, filled with impatience. He would have to wait until daylight before he could do anything else.

He turned in on a bunk in an empty cell and, despite the niggling thoughts in his mind, soon fell asleep, exhausted by the activities of the past twenty-four hours. It was just after dawn when he awoke, and he stretched and arose. The jail was quiet. Hank Tupp was asleep in his cell, breathing heavily through his gaping mouth, but the girl was awake, sober-faced and worried, seated on the foot of her bunk. She gazed forlornly at Manning, who felt a pang of sympathy for her.

'Can I trust you not to run away if I turn you loose?' he asked.

'I got nowhere to run to. I can't leave my grandfather.'

Manning fetched the cell keys and unlocked the door of the girl's cell. Hank Tupp awoke and got up. He staggered to the barred door of his cell and peered suspiciously at Manning, yawning and scratching himself.

'What's going on?' he demanded.

'There's no one else on duty,' Manning told him. 'Beth can get us breakfast. Miles will be coming back on duty later and I'll be riding out.' He studied Tupp's lined face. 'You had time to think things over?' he queried.

'I got nothing to say.' The old man turned away and sat on the foot of his bunk. 'You don't believe anything I do say,' he accused.

'You're a fool, Grandpa,' the girl said. 'You shouldn't be in here. You're going to take the rap for everyone else. Aitken turned everyone else loose but he left you in here to take whatever is coming to you. Tell the Ranger what he wants to know.'

'How can I tell him what I don't know?' Tupp shook his head doggedly and stretched out on his bunk.

The girl gazed at her grandfather for a moment, shaking her head in frustration. Then she uttered a cry of exasperation. Manning waited for more, but she turned and hurried into the office with tears in her eyes.

Manning followed her. 'Mebbe you'll tell me your side of it,' he suggested. 'I guess you know what was going on out at Double M.'

'I don't know much. Those rustlers showed up one day, and stayed until you came. There was always one of them hanging around, to keep an eye on us. Grandpa didn't seem to be in cahoots with them. They pushed him around some, when he didn't do as they said. But I'm sure he knew them.'

Manning nodded. 'I'll take a chance on you,' he decided, although he had no grounds for holding her under arrest. 'You can have the run of this place while Hank is behind bars. It might be better for you to stay here.'

'I got no place else to go,' she replied.

'There's an eating house along the street. I reckon the law office has an arrangement with them for supplying meals to the prisoners. Go along there and inform them that we need three breakfasts.'

The girl nodded and departed. Manning went out back to take a closer look at the hoofprints he had seen there. The sun was clear of the horizon now and he checked the ground thoroughly. There was a patch near the back door of the jail that was hard packed by trampling hooves, but a couple of yards out from the building he saw where five horses had set out fast across the back lots. He nodded, impatient to take up the trail.

When he returned to the front office the girl was waiting, and there was a large tray on the desk containing three plates of food, a coffee pot and three tin cups.

'The big plate is yours,' the girl told him. 'Prisoners get less food.'

Manning grinned and led the way into the cell block. The girl gave her grandfather his breakfast and a mug of coffee, and then sat opposite Manning at the desk in the office. Manning was in a hurry now, and soon finished his food. He drank two cups of coffee and got to his feet. Pacing the office, he was impatient for the jailer to arrive, and was pleased when the man eventually showed up.

Going to the stable, Manning saddled his horse and rode across the back lots to the rear of the jail. He checked his supplies and ammunition, then rode out on the trail of the escaped prisoners. They could run from him but they could not hide, and he had the patience of experience to see him through. He settled himself for a long ride, and the tracks stretched out before him like a beckoning finger. He still had no clear idea of what was happening in this county, but he was certain that it would not be long before he got within shooting distance of the guilty men.

By noon he was definitely riding south, and for a mile or two he toyed with the idea that Keno Jackson was leading the others towards the distant Mexican border. But then the tracks veered south-west, and from his study of the map of the county on the wall of the law office, Manning guessed that Jackson was making for the Slashed T.

By mid-afternoon he was passing small herds of grazing cattle, and there were other tracks in the short grass. A rider appeared in the distance and Manning sought cover. He hid in some brush until the rider passed, but continued to watch the man, noting that he was studying the ground.

It looked like the man had been sent to backtrack Jackson's trail, and within a few minutes of passing Manning's position he spotted Manning's fresh tracks and reined in. When he turned slowly to face Manning's hiding place, Manning drew his gun and rode into the open. He was twenty yards from the rider, and the man quickly held up his hands.

Manning gigged his mount in close and opened his vest to reveal his Ranger badge. 'Who are you and what are you doing?' he asked.

'I'm Jim Loomis. I ride for Slashed T.

I'm on my way to check the line cabin over on Lone Pine Creek.'

'You were backtracking the prints I've followed from town,' Manning accused. 'You saw my prints and that stopped you.'

'I saw the tracks and wondered who made 'em, and saw the fresh single prints following them. I was wondering who had the nerve to ride on Slashed T range. We don't get many strangers this side of the boundary. Visitors are plumb discouraged.'

'I can believe that. Have you come from the ranch?'

'Yep.' Loomis cut off whatever else he was going to say, and Manning nodded.

'So you must have seen the riders who left the tracks I'm following. They're heading into Slashed T. Who did you see?'

Before Loomis could answer a rifle cracked echoingly somewhere in the distance, and a moment later the bullet whined past Manning's head. He dived out of his saddle, and Loomis was not slow in following suit. Manning maintained his grip on his sixgun, and was still facing Loomis when he hit the ground. Loomis pulled his gun as he landed on both feet and swung the weapon to cover Manning.

'Don't try it,' Manning warned but the man kept moving, his face showing desperation. Manning levelled his Colt and fired, aiming for the man's right shoulder, and, as he fired, another bullet from the distant sniper smashed into his left thigh.

Manning twisted sharply, clenching his teeth against the pain that slashed through his leg. He rolled into better cover, aware that his bullet had dusted the shoulder of his target. Loomis was out of action. Manning clenched his teeth and eased himself into a more comfortable position, waiting stoically for developments while the gun echoes faded and grumbled away into the deep space of the illimitable range.

8

Manning could see gunsmoke drifting from a nearby ridge but there was no sign of the sniper who had shot him. He glanced at Loomis and saw that he was apparently unconscious, with blood showing on his right shoulder. Placing his sixgun near to hand, he eased himself into deeper cover and examined his left thigh. The wound was painful, and he feared it had crippled him, but when he saw the deep gouge through the flesh midway between the knee and the hip he realized that he had been lucky. The thigh bone had not been touched, and he quickly stripped off his neckerchief, shook the dust from it, and bound it around his thigh over his pants, ensuring that it covered the seeping wound.

Taking up his gun again, and favouring his left leg, he eased up to check his surroundings and saw a rider coming down off the high ground from where the shots had been fired. He glanced at Loomis to check that he was not going to be a problem and saw that he was now conscious but making no attempt to regain his gun.

'Loomis,' Manning called, 'pick up your gun by the barrel and toss it over here.'

Loomis obeyed and then slumped, overcome by the effort of moving. Manning warned him to remain motionless and edged away from the spot where he had fallen. It was obvious the sniper figured he had scored a telling hit and was coming to inspect his kill. Ignoring the pain in his thigh, Manning returned to where his horse stood with trailing reins. It was grazing peacefully, and he swung into the saddle, grunting at the pain he inflicted upon himself. He was covered from the rider by the brush surrounding him, and moved away in a small arc as the man approached. The newcomer was riding at a walk, rifle ready in his capable hands, the barrel resting on his saddlehorn and pointing slightly to his left. The newcomer called to Loomis but there was no reply.

Manning waited until the rider had passed, then gigged his mount forward out of cover.

'Hold it right there,' he called, cocking his gun.

The newcomer was at a disadvantage, his rifle pointing away from Manning. He reined in and threw a glance across his shoulder, and Manning felt a thread of pleasure unwind in his mind at the sight of the tense face peering at him. It was Jenson.

'This is a small world, huh?' Manning called. 'I trailed you and the others from the back of the jail.'

'You got more lives than a cat, Ranger,' Jenson snarled.

'I need 'em with men like you around.' Manning smiled coldly. He glanced around, checking his surroundings. The range seemed deserted now.

‘Where’s Jackson?’ he asked.

‘At the ranch. With you on the prowl he figgered this job was played out so we’re quitting cold. He reckoned you’d get on our trail so I back-trailed to take care of you.’

‘He should’ve figured you ain’t good enough to do that. Drop the rifle and shuck your sixgun. Don’t make any sudden move.’

He waited until Jenson had complied then made him dismount. Taking a set of handcuffs out of a saddle-bag he tossed them to Jenson.

‘Cuff your right wrist,’ Manning ordered, and Jenson obeyed reluctantly. ‘How are you feeling now, Loomis?’ he asked, aware that the wounded man was pressing his left hand against his right shoulder in an attempt to staunch the bleeding from his wound.

‘I’ll live, I reckon,’ came the harsh reply.

‘Well get up in your saddle. You mount up too, Jenson.’ Manning waited until they had obeyed. ‘Get up on the right, Loomis. That's it. Jenson, cuff Loomis's left wrist.'

Jenson looked as if he wanted to disobey, but the black eye of Manning's steady sixgun convinced him to do as he was told. He snapped the empty cuff on Loomis's left wrist and waited stoically for what was to follow.

'How far is it to Slashed T?' Manning demanded.

'Five miles, more or less,' Jenson replied.

'I can't ride far with my shoulder,' Loomis protested.

'I got a slug in my leg but I ain't complaining,' Manning told him unfeelingly.'

'You figger to ride into Slashed T?' Jenson gazed at Manning in wonder. 'They'll chew you and spit you out baldheaded.'

'Cut the gab and get moving,' Manning rapped.

They moved on, and Manning kept his prisoners several yards ahead, where he could watch them and the tracks he had been following. He had no predetermined plan of action but his method had always been to keep the pressure on the badmen. He grimaced in pain when he instinctively shifted his position in the saddle and the thigh wound protested sharply.

It was evening when he sighted Slashed T sprawled out on the range. There was a two-storey house beside a narrow creek, a low bunkhouse, two corrals, a barn and six other buildings arranged around a dusty yard. Reining up in cover, Manning took a pair of field glasses from his saddle-bag and studied the scene.

He noted a dozen horses in the corrals, and saw a man armed with a rifle lounging in the area of the barn. There were two men seated on a bench outside the bunkhouse and three figures sitting on the porch of the house, all heavily armed.

Quite a reception party, Manning mused. Jackson would expect pursuit, having busted jail, and he probably figured on a posse arriving. It looked as if he meant to stand and fight. Manning glanced at the sky. The sun was low on the distant horizon and night would fall in about an hour. He nodded, wanting to move in under cover of darkness to check out the situation more closely.

He moved back two hundred yards into deep cover, favouring his injured leg, and made dry camp. Neither prisoner desired food so he ate alone, and quenched his thirst with water from his canteen, not daring to light a fire to make coffee. Afterwards he prepared for his nocturnal foray. He tethered the horses in the copse then considered his prisoners. Loomis no longer complained about his shoulder wound. Manning examined it and saw that the bleeding had stopped.

He figured the man could manage until they eventually reached town, and made both men sit with a tree between them, their handcuffed hands behind the trunk. Then he took a pair of leg irons from his saddle-bag and shackled their ankles with the tree between them, securely anchoring them to one spot.

'I don't have to warn you not to make any noise, do I?' he asked when he was ready to leave. Night was closing in and a cool breeze rustled through the trees. 'And you better start praying that I don't get shot, because if I do you'll be in poor straits.'

Both men protested as he took his horse and departed but he ignored their pleas and continued. He rode through the growing darkness, moving slowly, and followed a route he had selected earlier, approaching the ranch from the rear. He had seen a dry wash which looked as if it would afford good cover to within a hundred yards of the ranch house, and, by the time he reached the vantage point he had selected, full darkness had fallen.

Manning removed a dozen leather thongs from a saddle-bag and hung them around his neck, tying the ends together. Each thong was roughly two feet in length. He had learned from hard experience that when he operated against a gang of badmen he would eventually need something to bind a prisoner and keep him out of the action without supervision. He left his horse in cover and moved slowly until he reached the rear of the house, which was in total darkness.

He found the back door locked and went to the right until he was standing at the rear corner, and when he looked along the side of the building he saw a large lighted window near the front corner. A man was standing on the near side of the window, the issuing light throwing his tall figure into silhouette.

The man was smoking, and Manning could see a rifle in his left hand. He had been expecting to find a guard, and he stood for some minutes, listening intently for sounds of other prowlers. Hearing nothing untoward, he steeled himself to move on.

His leg wound had stiffened considerably and was painful when he put his full weight upon the limb. He eased his sixgun from its holster and took a pace towards the guard, then another when the man gave no sign of sensing his presence. Step by step he moved towards the unsuspecting man, restraining his breathing as he edged to within four feet of the lighted window, his tension giving him the extra edge he needed.

He could hear the guard muttering, and then the man flicked away the butt of his cigarette, which flew in a tiny red arc through the darkness. Manning stepped forward quickly and jammed the muzzle of his Colt against the man's spine.

'Hold it,' he rasped softly. 'If you make a sound it'll be your last.'

The man gasped in shock but obeyed instantly, his hands lifting shoulder high. Manning slid a sixgun out of the man's holster and stuck it into the back of his own belt, where it nestled comfortably against his spine. He took the rifle from the man's left hand and propped it against the wall of the house, then slammed the barrel of his Colt against the man's skull and caught him as he slumped to the ground.

He rolled the man on to his back, and the light from the nearby window afforded him a look at the man's rough features. He was pleased to see that he had captured Spence. Manning quickly bound the man's hands then removed Spence's neckerchief, which he forced between Spence's teeth until he was effectively gagged.

Satisfied that Spence was safely out of it, Manning moved to the lighted window and risked a look into the room. It was deserted, obviously Dallas Thorpe's office. There was a desk inside, and a big safe in a corner. Ducking below the sill, he moved to the front corner of the house and squatted beside the porch, checking out the entire yard before turning his attention to the porch. There was no sign of another guard anywhere but he did not accept that one was not present.

There were two men sitting on the

porch and the low mumble of their voices easily reached Manning's ears. He listened for some moments, keen to pick up what information he could about the situation here at Slashed T, but could make nothing of their conversation. They were chatting generally about ranch work, and Manning waited, unable to continue while the porch was occupied.

After some minutes the front door of the house opened and a big figure appeared. Manning squinted his eyes to make out details, but it was not until the man spoke that he recognized Keno Jackson's arrogant voice.

'Blaney, saddle up and ride into town and listen around. I wanta know what that Ranger is figuring. He ain't followed my tracks from jail or he would have been here by now.'

'Heck, Spence and Jenson were with you in town. They know more about what's going on there than me. Send one of them.'

'I need those two to back me,'

Jackson replied. 'Jenson is out there watching for a posse and he won't be back till dawn. So ride out. With Thorpe away I need to know what's happening.'

'Thorpe should be back soon,' Blaney protested. 'He said he wouldn't be staying in town longer than to talk to his boss.'

Manning frowned. Thorpe had a partner in town? He shook his head. If that were true then a totally different situation existed from the one he had been considering. And who could be bossing murder and rustling from town?

'I need to know things,' Jackson snarled, his harsh voice cutting through Manning's racing thoughts. 'There could be a big posse on its way out from town right now. This whole deal looks like it's falling to pieces now the Ranger is in the county. So high-tail it into town. Find out what's going on and then come back. Price, go chase Hilton outa the bunkhouse and tell him to come here. I got the feeling all hell is about to break loose, and my hunches never let me down. We oughter be moving out before it's too late.'

'Before Thorpe gets back from town?' demanded Price.

'Thorpe owns this place so he's got to stick with it through hell and high water. We're different. All we need is the pay that's due to us and we can up stakes and pull out. Thorpe can face the music on his own. Now both of you get moving.'

'You ain't gonna pull out before I get back from town, are you?' Blaney demanded.

'If you stop yapping like a dog and get riding you'll be back before I'm ready to pull out,' Jackson retorted.

Both men arose and moved off the porch. Manning watched them until the darkness of the yard swallowed them. He heard the door of the house close and looked round. Jackson had gone back inside. He moved to the lighted window again, and saw Jackson entering the office. The big man walked to the safe in the corner and kicked it in frustration, then turned to the desk and sat down, helping himself to a drink from a whisky bottle standing on a tray.

Manning went back to the side of the porch and waited. A few tense moments passed and then he heard the sound of boots scuffing through the dust of the yard. A man appeared and stamped on to the porch. When he entered the house, Manning returned to the window. The man appeared in the doorway of the office and Jackson arose and went to the safe, where the newcomer joined him. They chatted at some length but Manning could not hear what was being said. Then the man nodded and departed. Manning watched him cross the yard again, and followed at a distance.

The man went into the bunkhouse and Manning circled it swiftly and made for the corrals. He heard movement; the stamp of restless hooves, the cursing of the man who had been detailed to ride into town. Manning drew his gun and went forward boldly.

'Blaney,' he called

'Who's that?'

'Jackson's changed his mind. You don't have to ride into town now.' Manning moved in towards the sound of Blaney's voice. He could just see the man. Blaney was standing with his saddle in his arms, peering towards Manning in an attempt to recognize him. But because Manning approached openly he was not suspicious. Manning reached him and swung his right fist in a whirling arc. His hard knuckles cracked against the side of Blaney's chin with a meaty sound and the man's legs buckled. Manning caught him and lowered him to the ground. In a moment Blaney was bound and gagged, and Manning dragged him into the shadows surrounding one of the huts near the corral.

Walking back to the house, Manning angled to the side of the bunkhouse and risked a look through one of the end windows, which was open. The lamplight inside the low building was dim, but he saw six men inside. Three were seated at a table, playing cards. Two more were stretched out on their bunks, and another, Hilton, who had been across to the house to talk with Jackson, was looking through a saddle-bag at one end of the long table.

Manning saw several sticks of dynamite on the table, and Hilton was producing caps and fuse wire from the bag.

'You figgerin' to blow a safe?' a card player demanded.

'I don't know what Jackson's got in mind, but he ain't in a good mood, and that could mean trouble for everyone,' Hilton retorted.

Manning turned away and returned to the house. Drawing his gun, he entered silently. He flung open the door to the office and stepped inside, covering Jackson as the ramrod looked up. Jackson's expression changed swiftly. He sprang to his feet, his right hand on the butt of his gun.

'Hold it,' Manning rapped, waggling his gun. 'You're on a knife edge, Jackson.'

The big man froze, then shrugged and dropped his hands to his sides. 'Looks like it's your deal,' he observed.

'You can bet your life on that. Put your hands up and turn around.' He went forward when Jackson had complied and relieved the man of his weapons. 'You should have kept going when you got out of jail,' he added. 'Now you're on your way back to a cell and this time Aitken ain't alive to help you out.'

'You killed Charlie Aitken?' Jackson's eyes narrowed and he clenched his big hands.

'He figured to kill me but lost out. You reckoned to cut your losses around here and run, huh? Where's Thorpe?'

'He ain't around. You ain't got a hope of getting away from here. Spence is out on guard, watching for trouble. And

Jenson is prowling around somewhere. He'll cut your sign for sure. He's itching to kill you after the way you took him for killing Corder.'

'Spence and Jenson are under arrest again.' Manning grinned at Jackson's evident surprise. 'Who's the boss Thorpe is in town to see?'

Jackson laughed but his big hands were clenched and his narrowed eyes were bleak-expressioned and alert, watching for the any lapse in Manning's concentration. 'So you've been sneaking around and uncovering things, huh?' He laughed again. 'Well, if you're so smart you should be able to figure it out.'

'I will in time. But first I got some cleaning up to do around here, and I'm starting with you.' Manning pulled one of the thongs from around his neck. 'Turn around. I'm gonna tie your hands. Then I'll wait for Hilton to come and blow Thorpe's safe and take him. After that I'll arrest the men in the bunkhouse, and that should take care of this place until Thorpe returns.'

'That ain't gonna be as easy as you figure.' Jackson scowled as he turned slowly under the menace of Manning's gun.

Manning raised his sixgun to deliver a blow to Jackson's head but the big ramrod had been waiting for that precise moment and pivoted back towards Manning, his right elbow jutting in an attempt to make contact with Manning's gunhand and force it out of alignment with his heavy body. Manning was ready for anything, but his response was a split second behind Jackson's move. The ramrod's right forearm struck Manning's gunhand, forcing it outwards, and the big man spun and delivered a heavy left hand punch to Manning's unprotected jaw.

Manning rolled with the punch, which grazed his chin, moving instinctively, his concentration on his gunhand. Jackson managed to get a grip on Manning's wrist and began forcing the weapon upwards. He threw another left hand punch and Manning lowered his head and took the blow on his right brow. Blood began to flow immediately, and he countered with his own left, smacking it flush against Jackson's chin.

The big ramrod sagged and Manning struck again, then lifted his left knee, slamming it into Jackson's groin. The man groaned and twisted away, and Manning jerked his gunhand free and crashed the barrel of the Colt against Jackson's left temple. Jackson groaned and dropped to the floor.

Manning backed off, breathing heavily, then holstered his gun and quickly bound Jackson's hands with a thong. Leaving Jackson lying behind the desk, he went to the front door, and as he opened it a figure came on to the porch.

'I got the dynamite,' Hilton said. 'You want I should do the job now?'

Manning palmed his gun and jabbed the hard muzzle into Hilton's stomach, easing back the hammer as he did so.

Hilton dropped the sack he was carrying and Manning grasped his shoulder.

'Pick up the dynamite and let's go into the office,' he rapped. 'Don't try anything or you're dead.'

'What's going on?' Hilton demanded. 'Who are you?'

'A Texas Ranger. Get moving.' Manning pushed open the door at his back and ushered Hilton into the house. He paused in the act of closing the front door, for the sound of distant thunder out there in the night came to his ears, which rapidly grew in volume and came speedily nearer.

Manning froze as he listened. At least half a dozen riders were hammering along the trail towards the ranch, and he knew with cold realization that he had run out of time. Thorpe was coming back from town, and this was where the showdown started.

9

Manning was tense as he hurried Hilton into the office. He struck the man with his gun, stunning him, and then tied him. By the time he straightened, riders were coming into the yard. He went to the front door and opened it a fraction, peering out into the starlit night. Six riders had turned off to the corral, but two were coming towards the house. Manning closed the door and went back into the office, drawing his Colt and checking the weapon.

The two riders reined in at the porch. Manning heard the thump of feet as they dismounted. Holstering his gun, he waited, and heard Thorpe's harsh voice as the rancher opened the front door.

'Make us some coffee, Jack.' The rancher's boots thudded on the board floor as he approached the office.

Manning glanced down at the two bound men and the sack of explosives Hilton had brought in. He eased his gun in its holster then relaxed, standing in a position that kept him out of line with the window. He faced the door and saw the handle turn. The door opened and Thorpe appeared. The rancher halted when he saw light in the office, and then his gaze alighted on Manning's grim figure. A host of expressions fled across the rancher's hard face, and Manning noted that sudden fear was the first of them.

'What in tarnation are you doing here? What's going on?' Thorpe demanded.

'I'm doing my job.' Manning smiled. He pointed at the two bound figures lying behind the desk and Thorpe craned forward until he could see Jackson and Hilton. 'I followed Jackson's tracks from town, and it's a good thing I got here when I did. These two were fixing to blow your safe with the dynamite in that gunny sack. It looks like you were about to lose your ramrod and some of your crew. I also got Spence tied up outside this window and Blaney hogtied over by the corral.'

Thorpe stood motionless for a moment, his narrowed eyes filled with calculation. He had been badly shocked to find Manning in his office, and even harder hit by the evidence of Jackson's perfidy. Manning remained silent, giving the rancher time to recover. In his own mind, Manning realized that he would be extremely fortunate to leave the ranch with his prisoners. But if he allayed Thorpe's fears for his own safety then there was a chance that the rancher would grasp at an opportunity to put himself in the clear.

'It's lucky for me you showed up,' Thorpe said at last. 'So Jackson decided to cut his losses and high-tail it after cleaning me out, huh?'

'That looks to be the way of it.' Manning's reflexes were hair-triggered. 'In town you said you would be ready to back the law if it needed help. I want my prisoners collected and roped to their saddles so I can take them back to jail.'

'I'll give you all the help I can.' Thorpe replied.

Manning knew that Thorpe could not let him take anyone back to town, and he was ready for the first hostile move on the rancher's part. But Thorpe gave no indication of concern. He turned to the door and opened it.

'Jack' he called, and a man appeared. 'Go over to the bunkhouse and tell some of the men to saddle up — ' He paused and glanced at Manning. 'How many prisoners have you got?'

'Four,' Manning said.

Thorpe nodded and permitted himself a faint grin. 'Tell them to saddle four horses. They'll find Blaney hogtied over by the corral. He's to be tied to his saddle and brought here. Spence is outside the office window, likewise hogtied. He's going back to jail as well. And there's Jackson and Hilton here in the office. The Ranger stopped them blowing my safe and high-tailing it with my cash.'

Jack's face was showing the extent of his shock but he hurried off without hesitation. Thorpe turned to Manning.

'It'll be taken care of,' he said. 'You can relax now. How about a drink?'

'No thanks.' Manning shook his head. 'I'll need to keep my wits about me with half a dozen prisoners to haze along. I picked up Jenson and Loomis back on the trail and they're handcuffed to a tree, waiting for my return.'

'You sure have been busy. But that's the way the Rangers work, huh?'

'We do have a reputation.' Manning checked Jackson's bonds. The ramrod was sneering at him, and Manning knew he was expecting Thorpe to outwit the law. No matter what friction or problems existed between these badmen, they had to unite against the law or face the prospect of arrest and jail.

Minutes later the sound of hooves in

the yard became apparent and someone called the house. Manning drew his gun and made Jackson and Hilton get to their feet. Jackson threw a questioning glance at Thorpe, which Manning did not miss, and Thorpe frowned and shook his head in reply. Manning picked up the sack containing the explosives.

The prisoners were taken outside, and Manning saw half a dozen tough gunnies standing around the four horses that had been saddled. Blaney was roped to the saddle of one horse, and at that moment two men appeared with Spence between them. They quickly thrust him up into a saddle and roped him securely. Jackson and Hilton were similarly handled. No one spoke, and Manning was wondering when Thorpe would make his move.

'Is there anything else I can do for you?' Thorpe asked. 'Do you need a couple of men to ride with you in case of trouble on the trail?'

'No thanks. I can manage from here

on in.' Manning went around his prisoners, ensuring that they were securely tied, then roped the horses together.

'Where's your horse? Thorpe demanded.

'Behind the house.'

'Jack, fetch the Ranger's horse.' Thorpe waited until the man had moved to obey then confronted Manning, and for a moment Manning thought matters were coming to a head. 'I guess I got to thank you for catching these polecats before they could blow my safe,' he said. 'I figure they were responsible for most of the trouble that's occurred on the range. It was a clever trick for them to work for an honest rancher while raising hell in other parts.'

'Thanks.' Manning nodded. He took the reins of his horse when it was brought to the front of the house and swung into the saddle. Thorpe handed him the end of the rope linking the horses of the prisoners together and

Manning wound it around his saddle-horn.

He was tense, his back muscles bunched in anticipation of a shot, as he rode around the corner of the house and set off on the long trip to town. But there was silence in the yard, and he could not believe that Thorpe would allow him to ride clear. But perhaps the rancher did not want bloodshed in his own yard, and Manning knew he would have to be on his guard every minute of the trip to town.

He did not feel any easier when he had drawn clear of Slashed T because his subconscious mind was pricking him, trying to convey some message to him. He reined in and dismounted, then tied his horse and those of the prisoners securely to a tree.

'I'll come back and gutshoot anyone who makes a sound,' he warned his prisoners, and turned abruptly and started running back towards the rear of the ranch house. His left leg protested painfully but he kept moving, and was gasping for breath when he heard the sound of hooves just ahead, coming from the rear of the house. He halted and dropped to one knee, his sixgun sliding into his right hand.

A rider was coming towards him, moving at a canter, and Manning nodded to himself. Here was the trouble he had been expecting. Thorpe had sent one of his gunnies to shoot him in the back and turn the prisoners loose. But Manning had other ideas. He was about to put another kink in Thorpe's rope.

Manning waited until the rider was almost upon him before he sprang upright. The horse shied nervously and Manning grabbed for the nearest rein, hauling on it and thrusting the muzzle of his gun under the rider's nose.

'Get out of the saddle,' Manning rasped.

The man obeyed, and Manning struck him heavily with the barrel of his gun. The man slumped to the ground and Manning struck again, hitting him across the forehead.

With no time to spare, Manning set off again, running to the rear of the house. He paused for breath when he reached it, then moved around the rear corner and went towards the porch, ducking under the lighted office window. He went into a crouch by the front corner, and eased forward to look along the porch.

Thorpe was standing on the porch and there were half a dozen riders facing him in the yard, the light from a nearby window outlining their hard faces. Thorpe was talking harshly, and Manning caught the tail-end of what was being said.

'So we've finished pussy-footing around. I want you six to ride over to Double M and hold it for me. We're taking over completely on this range. Mason will kill the Ranger before he can get the prisoners back to town, and he'll finish off Jackson and those who have thrown in with him and arrange things so it will look like Jackson killed the Ranger. Jackson will get the blame and we'll be in the clear. Now get moving. I want to be in control by dawn.'

The riders wheeled their mounts and cantered away across the yard. Thorpe stood for a moment, then turned and entered the house. Manning remained motionless, his thoughts fleeting as he considered the development. For a moment he was undecided about his immediate actions. Then he went to the office window and peered in. Thorpe was seated at his desk, drinking whisky, and Manning sneaked away, heading back to his prisoners.

He found Mason still out cold, his horse standing nearby with trailing reins. He bound Mason's hands and slung him across his saddle, then went on, leading the horse. When he came up with his four prisoners he checked their bonds and found them still secure. Mounting his buckskin, he continued until he came to the stand of trees where he had left Jenson and Loomis and quickly transferred them to their horses. Then he rode on, moving through the starlit night, following the trail that led to town and determined to get there with his prisoners no matter what tactics Thorpe tried.

Despite the fact that because he had taken Mason there seemed to be no immediate threat to him, Manning did not relax his vigilance. He estimated that twenty miles separated him from town, and he kept his party moving steadily. He paused once to check Mason, found the man conscious, and roped him in his saddle in a sitting position. Then he continued.

After an hour's riding he made a halt to give the horses a breather. Jackson had been complaining during the last half hour and Manning went to his side.

'Stop bellyaching, Jackson. I'm suffering on this ride too, but it will be over for all of you by dawn.'

'You ain't got your hands tied,' Jackson countered.

'There's nothing I can do about that, so quit beefing.' Manning went around the group, rechecking bonds.

He found that Jenson had loosened the rope around his wrists, and untied the knot to tighten it. The next instant Jenson's knee came up, his foot leaving the stirrup, and slid up Manning's chest before connecting with his chin, sending him reeling. Manning fell back against one of the other riders, who also kicked at him, and then sprawled heavily on the ground.

Before Manning could recover, Jenson had shaken off his rope and dived from his saddle, He landed heavily on Manning's back, pushing him against the ground with a force that knocked the breath from him. Manning was dazed, and in the split second when he was unable to move, Jenson was reaching for Manning's holstered sixgun.

The sound of the gun rasping from its holster alerted Manning to his danger and he twisted on to his back beneath Jenson, his right hand clawing for a grip on his sixgun. His long fingers closed around Jenson's wrist and he exerted his strength as Jenson jerked the gun clear of leather. At the same time he smashed his left fist upwards into the dark mass that was Jenson's head, and his knuckles cracked against the man's forehead. Striking again, Manning caught Jenson flush in the right eye. The gunnie hurled himself sideways to avoid the full force of the blow, and Manning arched his back and dug his heels into the grass, twisting his body to dislodge the killer.

Jenson fell sideways. Manning tightened his grip on the man's right wrist, trying desperately to force the muzzle of the gun skywards. The weapon exploded raucously and the reddish flame spurting from the muzzle tattered the darkness of the night. The bullet crackled past Manning's left ear, and the heavy report set his ears ringing. He maintained his hold on Jenson's gun wrist, twisting to keep the man in front of him.

Jenson could not break Manning's grip. He sledged his left fist into Manning's face, and Manning thought part of the sky had fallen on him. Shaking his head, Manning replied with his own left, and crashed his knuckles into Jenson's mouth. He could hear Jenson sobbing for breath from his exertions, and called upon all of his strength to end the fight. Jenson used his left hand in an attempt to break Manning's grip and Manning butted his head forward, smashing his forehead against Jenson's nose.

The killer twisted away, loosening his grip, and Manning surged upright, pulling Jenson with him. He ripped his gun from Jenson's grasp, ducking to the right as Jenson threw another left to his jaw. The knuckles landed against Manning's temple and his legs buckled. He almost went down, but shook his head and jabbed the muzzle of his gun into Jenson's stomach.

Jenson slumped to the ground in

defeat, and Manning slammed his gun barrel against the man's head, stunning him. Pushing himself erect, Manning stood with whirling senses and ringing ears. He looked over the other prisoners and was relieved to see them sitting quietly in their saddles, still securely roped.

Manning holstered his gun and lifted Jenson bodily. He threw the man across his saddle and roped him face down. Rechecking the bonds of each prisoner again, he wearily rode on.

Dawn was greying the sky when Manning finally spotted Oaktown. He eased his aching body and straightened his weary shoulders, then twisted to glance back at his prisoners, wincing when his left thigh protested at the movement. He rode into town and continued along the street to the jail, the hoofbeats of his little cavalcade echoing around the huddled buildings.

There were several men on the sidewalks. The storekeeper was sweeping off the front of his store, and a rider was coming along the street from the opposite direction. Manning eyed the newcomer, forcing himself to full alertness. He recognized Doc Hoyt, and reined in as the medico drew level with him.

'Looks like you've had a sleepless night,' Manning said.

'Yeah. And you've been busy. I'll bet you didn't get much sleep either.' Hoyt looked over the seven riders, nodding slowly as he recognized some of them. 'Looks like you've got back those who escaped from jail, plus a couple more.'

'I've got some work for you, Doc.' Manning eased his left foot out of the stirrup and tried to flex his muscles. The wound in his thigh had stiffened considerably. 'I got a man with a bullet wound in his shoulder.'

'I'll go back to the jail with you,' Hoyt replied.

Manning was relieved when he slid out of his saddle in front of the law office. Hoyt dismounted quickly and rapped on the door. Manning stood by his horse, waiting for the circulation in his leg to become normal. The office door was opened and the night jailer peered out, shotgun ready for trouble. He emitted a whoop of joy when he saw the huddled riders.

'Hell if you ain't brung back all them escaped prisoners,' he shouted. 'That's really somethin'. I never expected to see any of them again, or you, for that matter, Ranger. How'd you catch 'em? Did you put salt on their tails?'

'Cover them with your scattergun while I unite them,' Manning said. He eased his gun in its holster and went to work, freeing all seven prisoners. The gunnies filed into the law office and Miles took the keys and led the way into the cell block. Manning sighed with relief when the last of the prisoners was locked in a cell.

Doc Hoyt went into the cell where Loomis had stretched out on a bunk and began to attend to the man's wound. Miles stood guard at the door, and Manning went into the office and sat down heavily at the desk. He began to write a report of the incidents that had taken place, and looked up when the street door was opened. Beth Tupp entered the office. She paused at the sight of Manning, then came to stand beside the desk.

'I heard you riding in,' she said. 'You've got the prisoners back, and you look like you've been in a war.'

Manning fingered his battered face and nodded slowly. 'That's the way it goes in this job,' he replied. 'Has Hank decided to co-operate yet?'

'No. He's a stubborn old man. He won't lift a finger to help himself even though he knows he's facing years in jail.'

'You must know something of what went on out at Double M. Tell me and I'll go easy on Hank.'

She shook her head doubtfully, then opened her mouth to speak, but at that moment Hoyt and Miles came out of the cell block and she compressed her lips stubbornly. The jailer locked the door. Hoyt came to Manning's side, stifling a yawn and blinking his eyes rapidly.

'Loomis will be okay in a couple of weeks,' he opined. 'I guess I better take a look at you now. Have you been shot anywhere? There's blood on you here and there.'

Manning pushed back his chair and stretched out his left leg. 'I got nicked in the thigh,' he said. 'It hurts, but doesn't inconvenience me none.'

Hoyt removed the neckerchief Manning had tied around the wound, put his two index fingers in the bullet hole in the cloth of Manning's pants and ripped it to expose the blood-stained wound. The doc sent Beth to get some water, then bathed the wound.

'It ain't too serious, but you better keep it bound for a while to keep the dirt out. Can you stay out of your saddle for twenty-four hours?'

'I reckon to get some sleep before I consider my next move,' Manning replied, 'and I figger that might take all of twenty-four hours.'

Hoyt bandaged Manning's thigh and then departed. Manning went back to his report, and had practically finished it when breakfast for a dozen arrived from the eating house. Reaction began to fill him and he realized just how tired he was. He almost fell asleep over his meal, which he ate hurriedly. He drank several cups of strong coffee then pushed himself wearily to his feet.

'I'll take the horses to the livery barn, then come back here to sleep,' he told the jailer. 'Have you got someone to relieve you for the day?'

'Yeah, that's been taken care of. I telegraphed the sheriff in San Lorenzo yesterday and got a reply last night. He's sending a deputy over from the county seat. I reckon he should be arriving any time now. I'll go off duty when he shows up.'

Manning nodded and left the office. The sun was clear of the horizon now and the shadows had fled from the town. He looked around the wide street, breathing deeply of the crisp morning air. Tiredness had dulled his senses, but he fought against it and swung into the saddle of his buckskin. Taking up the rope linking the other seven horses together, he set off along the street to the livery barn.

Trying to consider his next move seemed to be too much for his tired mind, but he was aware that he had to move decisively before Dallas Thorpe realized that his plot to kill the Ranger and some of the prisoners had failed. He knew then that he had to go back to Slashed T as soon as possible and arrest Thorpe.

Despite his weariness, Manning's alertness was at full pitch, and when he heard a window in a nearby building scrape open a few inches his gaze was drawn to it. He located the window and narrowed his eyes against the glare of the rising sun. He heard hoofbeats approaching at that moment but dared not remove his gaze from the window. Was someone laying for him?

There was no movement at the window. A curtain veiled the interior of the room from his hard gaze. Then he saw a tiny movement in the four-inch gap, and when he saw a rifle barrel being eased forward into the gap he kicked his right foot clear of his stirrup, leaned to the left and dropped out of his saddle. As he hit the ground a rifle blasted, sending a string of echoes clear across town. He dimly heard the smack of a 40-40 slug striking the street within inches of where he lay, then the screeching whine as it ricocheted through the air.

Manning palmed his Colt and eased to one knee. His horse, although startled, moved only a few steps before standing with trailing reins. Manning threw up his gunhand. He could see a puff of blue smoke agitating around the window and fired swiftly, sending two slugs through the centre of the glass.

In the back of his mind was the thought that a party of riders was coming into town. He had heard their hooves as the shooting started. Now he risked a swift glance around and saw a party of riders, maybe a dozen, coming along the street from the stable end. He could not identify any of them at the distance, and dared not let his concentration be impaired. He checked out the window again, getting to his feet when no further shots were fired at him.

He started at a run across the street, making for the building from which the shot had been fired. A distant shout caught his attention and he glanced towards the approaching riders. They were coming at a gallop now, raising dust, and then a shot crashed out and a bullet whined over his head.

Manning left his horse and ran for cover. He gained an alley mouth and dived into it, with several bullets smacking into the surrounding woodwork. Gritting his teeth, his tiredness no longer evident, he started along the alley, determined to track down his ambusher. He reached the back lots, aware that one rider at least was now pursuing him, and flung himself at the back door of the house. It was locked and he stepped back a pace and then raised his foot to kick it in.

The sound of hooves was loud now, and Manning risked another look around. Riders were spilling out of the alley, and two were emerging from an alley further along the street. Sunlight flickered on drawn guns, and Manning clenched his teeth when he realized that he was outnumbered and cornered. He was tempted to try and kick in the back door to get away from the menace of the drawn guns but already some of the riders were covering him.

'Drop your gun and put your hands up high!' a harsh voice yelled at him. 'Do it now or you're dead!'

Manning dropped his gun and lifted his hands. A dozen guns were covering him and he froze into immobility. He gazed at taut faces, trying to recognize one which would point to the identity of this bunch but they were all strangers. He watched a big man come pacing towards him, sixgun levelled, face set in harsh lines. The man halted a few yards from Manning and reached into a vest pocket. He stuck something on the front of his shirt, and, when his hands moved away, Manning saw a six-pointed star glinting in the sunlight.

'You're a deputy sheriff?' Manning demanded.

'Name of Tom Smith,' came the harsh reply. 'I'm a deputy sheriff of this county. Sheriff Gauvin sent me and this posse over from San Lorenzo because trouble had busted out here, and it looks like we didn't get in any too soon. You look like you've been in a battle.'

'I'd say you got here just in time,' Manning replied. He opened his jacket to reveal his Ranger badge. 'Did the sheriff warn you there was a Ranger operating around here?'

'He sure did, and you're the guy, huh? So what's going on? We heard shooting as we came along the street.'

'Someone just took a shot at me from a upper window out front. I was about to call him to account, if he's still inside.'

Deputy Smith turned to the posse. 'Half of you get back to the street and cover the front of this place,' he ordered. 'No shooting unless you're shot at.'

Six of the riders moved off immediately to obey, and Smith picked up Manning's gun and handed it to him. Together they kicked at the door and smashed the lock. A woman appeared in an inner doorway as they entered and began screaming. Manning hurried to her side and thrust his law badge under her nose. He grasped her arm and shook her slightly.

'I was shot at from a front window, the far one on the left on the first floor.' he told her. 'Who lives in this house?'

'It's a rooming house,' she replied hesitatingly, 'and Sam Askew uses it when he stops over in town.'

'Askew!' Manning cuffed back his dusty Stetson.

'Ain't that the local lawyer?' said

Smith. 'Why would he wanta shoot at a Texas Ranger?'

'Let's go and ask him,' Manning responded. He led the way through the house and up the stairs, and Smith covered him while he tried the door, which was locked.

Smith stepped forward and kicked the flimsy door, which splintered inwards, and Manning saw at a glance that the room was deserted.

'He got out quick,' said Smith. 'Well there's nowhere he can hide in town.'

'Perhaps he's leaving.' Manning started for the stairs. He hurried out to the street and swung into his saddle. Wheeling his buckskin, he started at a run for the stable. Some of the possemen followed, sensing more shooting.

Manning rode into the stable and dismounted almost before his horse had halted. He looked around, hand on his holstered gun, and saw the liveryman cleaning out a stall. The man looked up at the clatter of Manning's hooves then came out of the stall and leaned on his fork.

'Has Sam Askew been here for a horse?' Manning asked.

'Nope. He was here last night though and saddled his black. Said he had to make an early start this morning and was gonna leave his horse in the shed back of Ma Thompson's rooming house.'

Manning turned and regained his saddle. He went back along the street and entered an alley to reach the rear lot behind the rooming house. There was a large shed standing at the rear, the door open, and Manning could see that it was empty. Smith emerged from the rear of the house and looked enquiringly at Manning, who explained what had happened. They walked together to the shed and checked the ground for prints.

'Yeah,' opined the deputy. 'Them's fresh tracks all right. Looks like Askew ran outa the house after the shooting, jumped in his saddle and lit out for other parts. I talked to Ma Thompson and she said Askew told her a few days ago that he wouldn't want the room after the end of this week. What do you want him for?'

'I don't know yet,' Manning replied. 'I'll have to take out after him. He's got some questions to answer, apart from shooting at me.'

'Want some of the posse to back you up?'

'No thanks. I always work alone. The best thing you can do is go to the jail and take over there. Read the reports I've written over the last couple of days and they'll fill you in on what's been going on. Arrest anyone who rides for Slashed T and hold them until I get back.' Manning paused and thought for a moment. 'If you can get out to Slashed T then I'd appreciate it if you arrested Thorpe himself. He's another with a lot of questions to answer.'

'Sure thing. Consider it done. You're gonna run down Askew, huh?'

'I'll get him,' Manning said softly,

and went back to his horse. He returned to the street and collected the horses the prisoners had ridden into town and went back to the stable.

He left his buckskin to be rested and grained properly, and rented a good horse from the stable. Minutes later he was back at the rear of the rooming house to pick up Askew's tracks, and then he set out once more on the trail with no thought in his mind beyond the fact that he had a chore to do.

10

Manning pushed along briskly when he was clear of town. The horse was fresh and ran freely, but he settled it down and chased it along the line of the tracks left by Askew's horse. With something definite to do, Manning's tiredness had fled, and he leaned forward grimly in the saddle and studied the way ahead as he galloped to the north-west.

Why had Sam Askew tried to kill him? The lawyer was practically the only man in the county who knew that the Texas Ranger and Chuck Manning were one and the same man. It obviously had to do with Double M, and Manning let his thoughts dwell upon the different aspects of the business that were opened up to him by the knowledge that Askew was somehow implicated.

While he rode he studied the ground ahead. Whenever he topped a rise he could see for miles, but although Askew's tracks led on and on he did not spot his quarry. Noon came, and he decided that Askew was heading for the Double M, which suited him, for the remaining questions bothering him could be answered on the range where his uncle had died.

Had Askew killed Uncle Mort? Was the lawyer in the business of buying up spreads? Dallas Thorpe had ridden into town the day before to confer with his boss. Was Askew that man?

Manning puzzled over the imponderable questions that reared in his mind, but did not relax his alertness, and when he spotted two riders ahead, coming steadily towards him, he eased his gun in its holster and held closely to the trail he was following. The two men came up fast, side by side, and were barely ten yards from Manning when they pulled their guns and started shooting at him.

Manning had been ready for trouble, and as the men made their play he pulled his horse to a halt and dismounted, his Colt in his hand as he planted his feet firmly on the grass. Bullets began crackling around him, and Manning ducked behind his horse. The animal ran to the left and Manning dropped to the ground, his big revolver lifting for action.

Bullets thudded into the ground around Manning, too close for comfort, but he ignored the fire. His teeth were clenched as he drew a bead on the nearer rider. He fired, and the man uttered a cry and pitched sideways out of leather, hitting the ground barely six feet in front of Manning. The horse ran on, leaping over Manning, who had already turned his attention to the second man.

The man had kicked his nearside foot out of its stirrup and was lying along the back of his horse as it thundered past Manning's position, his head down so that he could shoot at

Manning from under the neck of the galloping animal.

Manning swung his gun, leading his target, and gritted his teeth as he fired, for there was not much of the man to aim at. His bullet struck the speeding horse in the neck and the animal went down heavily in a bad fall. Its head dropped and hit the ground first, its body cartwheeling in a thresh of limbs. The rider was flung forward out of the saddle and hit the ground hard, and then the horse fell upon him. Manning grimaced as he cocked his gun. The heavy echoes of the shots were fading fast across the range, and he drew a quick breath. Gunsmoke dissipated on the stiff breeze.

Getting to his feet, Manning went forward to bend over the man lying inertly just in front of him. He could see the man was dead without touching him, and looked into a bearded face that belonged to a stranger. He straightened, his eyes narrowed, a weary frown upon his brow. Crossing to the fallen horse of the second rider, which was threshing wildly in the grass and squealing in pain, he fired a shot into the animal's brain to put it out of its misery and then turned his attention to the fallen rider.

The man was dead, his neck broken. But he was not a stranger. This was one of the rustlers from Double M, the man Manning had arrested at the ranch and brought to jail. He had been released by Aitken with the rest of the prisoners. Manning tried to recall the man's name, and then it came to him. Bill Jones.

Manning's thoughts were interrupted by the sudden rattle of hooves and he looked up quickly to see a rider fast disappearing into a draw ahead. It looked like Askew, and it appeared that the man had been watching the shooting. Manning hurried back to his horse, swung into the saddle and gave chase.

Hitting the draw, Manning peered ahead, expecting an ambush. Twice he saw the horse ahead, and became certain that the rider was Askew. He was gaining slowly on the man when the draw petered out on a ridge, Manning emerged from it to see the lawyer galloping on across the range, barely fifty yards ahead.

Manning reined in and slid his Winchester out of the saddle-boot. Jacking a 40-40 cartridge into the breech, he raised the weapon to his shoulder. Restraining his breathing, he drew a bead on the departing rider and fired. A moment later his quarry slumped in the saddle then fell forward over the neck of the horse. The animal slowed its pace but kept moving, and Manning gave chase, his ears ringing from the crack of the shot.

He overhauled the fleeing horse and was soon able to grab a rein and haul the animal to a halt. The rider was holding on to the horse's mane. It was Askew, Manning saw, and there was a splotch of blood on his right shoulder-blade. As the horse halted, Askew slid sideways and pitched to the grass, groaning.

Manning dismounted and thrust his rifle into its boot. He hunkered down over Askew, who was lying on his face, and pulled the man over on to his back. Askew seemed to be unconscious. There was blood dribbling from a corner of his mouth and his fleshy face looked ghastly grey. He was too old to be hammering around the range, Manning thought. He eased Askew into a more comfortable position and the man's eyes flickered open. Manning sat back on his heels and cuffed back his Stetson.

'I'm a mite surprised at this situation, Askew,' he said softly. 'Do you wanta tell me what brung you down to shooting at me and fleeing from the law?'

Askew looked up at him without comprehension, his eyes filled with shock, his brow wrinkled in a frown. Then his expression slowly cleared and his lips trembled as he made an effort to speak. 'You proved too good for me,' he muttered, his right hand lifting slowly to wipe blood from his mouth. 'I'm hit bad, I reckon. I can feel bleeding inside. You've done for me, Manning. I was a fool to figure Thorpe's crew could handle you. They sure made a mess of it. And it didn't take you long to bust my set-up out at Double M. I knew when you jailed Tupp that I was running out of time. Tupp would have spilled his guts to save himself when you got round to putting pressure on him.'

'So what happened before my arrival?' Manning asked. 'Who killed my uncle?'

'I did.' Askew spoke slowly, searching for the right words. 'But it wasn't meant to be like that. I didn't set out to kill him. I heard he was thinking of selling up and going back to Kansas so I rode out and asked him to sell to me. He told me he'd changed his mind because Thorpe had threatened trouble if Slashed T didn't get the Double M. So he was going to stay and fight.'

Askew's voice had been gradually sinking lower and lower, and he finally lapsed into silence, his eyes staring. Manning thought the lawyer was dead and shook him slightly. Askew stirred and some animation flowed into him. He lifted his head and turned it sideways and blood ran from a corner of his mouth.

'I kind of liked the idea of owning Double M,' he said thickly. 'And I was keen to put one over on Thorpe. I'd bought out a couple of other smaller ranchers ahead of Thorpe, which brought him bellowing into my office. Thorpe had been in the market for buying up spreads for some time. I knew, because I did his legal work. But Thorpe didn't want trouble with me so we entered into a partnership, and that's when Thorpe ran wild. He had plans to take over the whole county, and didn't care who got hurt in the process. I tried to keep a rein on him but he wouldn't listen to reason. He brought in some tough gunnies and started frightening everyone who stood in his way. But he could not get hold of Double M because you were on your way to take over.'

Again Askew fell silent, and his breath rattled in his throat. He moved his head from side to side, as if trying to get some air into his lungs. A red froth appeared on his lips and Manning grimaced.

'You got anything else on your mind you wanta tell me before you die?' he asked softly.

Askew opened his mouth to speak but a torrent of blood poured from between his lips. He stiffened, his hands clawing the air, and then he sighed long and harshly and slumped into death.

Manning got to his feet, his face harshly set. He looked around. The range was silent, empty. Getting his bearings, he stifled a sigh. He was close to Double M. He walked unsteadily to his horse and swung into the saddle, then went on towards his uncle's ranch.

When the cow spread came in sight, Manning reined in and studied the scene. There were half a dozen horses in the corral which were ready-saddled, and, even as he assessed the situation, three men emerged from the bunkhouse, went to the corral and began catching their mounts and tightening cinches. Manning watched until they were ready to ride, and when they departed towards the south he figured they were riding to Slashed T.

He recalled that he had overheard Thorpe's instructions to half a dozen men to ride to Double M and take over. They must have driven out the remaining rustlers Askew had brought in. Thinking it over, Manning touched spurs to his horse and started for the yard of the ranch, keeping an eye on the three departing riders until they vanished into the range. When he reached the gateway to the yard he saw four men emerging from the ranch house to range themselves side by side on the porch.

The men waited stolidly as Manning rode towards them. He reached a spot ten yards in front of the porch and reined in to step down from his saddle and trail his reins. He slapped the neck of his horse and sent it cavorting several feet to the right and out of the line of fire. Then he faced the four and walked in several feet, his right hand down at his side, apparently limp but in reality ready to reach for his holstered gun. His dark eyes were staring out over his taut, sunburned cheeks, holding a glint as harsh as sunlight on wind-swept ice.

The waiting men were silent and motionless, tense and wary, and there was about them an air of efficiency. They were cold-eyed, watching him unblinkingly, their features wooden, hands down at their sides, and two of the four were wearing crossed cartridge belts around their waists which supported twin sixguns. They waited stolidly, ready to earn their gun wages.

'Who's rodding this crew?' Manning's voice cracked like a whip.

One of the four was tall, lean, rawboned, with a long, horse-like face. The long white scar of a knife slash marred his right cheek. His Stetson was pushed back and black hair lay in a tangle on his forehead. He was wearing a sixgun on his right hip, and his right hand was close to the weapon, the thumb lying along the top of his cartridge belt.

'I'm the guy,' he said in a reedy voice. 'Pete Raynor. But I don't see that it's any of your damn business.'

'I'm making it my business,' Manning said quietly.

'You're the Ranger, ain't you?' one of the others cut in.

'You got it. That makes it my business. You're trespassing, and I'm giving you a choice. Get your horses, mount up and ride out, or pull your guns and start shooting.'

'Heck, I ain't taking on a Ranger,' the gunnie on the left said, his voice unsteady with tension. 'I don't get paid enough to handle that kind of chore.

What in hell has Thorpe gotten hisself into?'

'If you don't want gunplay then take out your gun and drop it,' Manning advised. 'Do it slow. If you others plan to make a stand then start it right now.'

The gunnie who quit took hold of his holstered gun with finger and thumb on the butt and eased it clear of greased leather. As he dropped it to the boards, Raynor made his play, and he was fast. His gun seemed to leap from its holster and level at Manning. Yet fast as he was, Manning's move was way ahead. His right hand moved in a blur, and red flame licked outwards from the lifting muzzle of his sixgun. Swift gunblasts shattered the silence.

Raynor did not finish his draw. His gun spilled out of his hand and he clutched at his chest, where blood began to spread quickly through the thin fabric of his shirt. The other two gunnies seemed to be drawn into the fight by Raynor's action. They slapped leather, and Manning turned his smoking weapon upon them. Two quick shots blasted the fading echoes of the initial shooting and both gunmen went down in a heap of threshing limbs, neither managing to fire a shot.

Manning stood motionless, his body wreathed in blue gunsmoke. His eyes were narrowed to the merest slits, and he motioned for the remaining gunman to move out. The man turned and went at a run towards the corral, and a moment later the sound of rapid hoofbeats pounded the hard ground as he high-tailed it for other parts.

Manning heaved a sigh and looked around as he reloaded the spent chambers of his gun. He kept the weapon in his hand as he went into the house and searched it, and nodded when he found it deserted. He went back outside to the porch and halted abruptly, for Dallas Thorpe and two gunnies were riding across the yard towards the house. Manning pulled the brim of his Stetson low over his eyes to cut down the glare of the sun. His sixgun was in its holster. He stood over the dead men on the porch, awaiting the arrival of the crooked rancher.

Thorpe raised himself in his stirrups and looked around. He called out as he approached, his harsh voice echoing around the yard.

'I heard shooting,' he said, not immediately recognizing Manning. 'What was that about?'

'It was me, cleaning up,' Manning replied.

Thorpe reined up yards from the porch. 'You!' he gasped, his expression turning bleak. He glanced at his two gunhands. 'He's the Ranger, you fools. Gun him down.'

Manning was watching all three of them, and when he saw one of the gunnies make a play for his gun he drew his own weapon and squeezed off a shot without seeming to take aim. The gunman yelled thinly and pitched sideways out of his saddle. The other gunman immediately raised his hands. Thorpe sat still in his saddle.

'Get rid of your guns,' Manning said. 'Do it slowly.'

The gunman obeyed with alacrity, easing his Colt clear of leather and dropping it to the ground. Thorpe looked as if he would disobey, but took his Colt from its holster and threw it to the ground.

'Now dismount.' Manning eased forward his hammer and holstered the weapon as both men stepped down into the dust. He motioned them to come forward, clear of their mounts.

'What are you doing here?' Thorpe demanded. 'The last time I saw you, you were on your way to town with several prisoners.'

'And you sent Mason after me.'

Thorpe's eyes narrowed. 'What happened to Mason?'

'I doubled back to your place and met him on his way. He's in jail with Jackson and the others. Are you ready to tell me what's been going on in this county?'

'I ain't done anything except protect

my property,' Thorpe blustered.

'That ain't what Askew told me before he died.'

A wary light shone in Thorpe's eyes. 'Askew's dead?'

'I got the rights of it from him, and no doubt some of my prisoners will be eager to tell me the rest of it when I get down to doing a deal with them. But one thing puzzles me, Thorpe. Why didn't Askew tell you about me when I rode in?'

'He did say a Ranger had ridden in.' Thorpe was frowning, wondering what was coming next.

'But he didn't tell you I am Chuck Manning. I own this place.' Manning was watching Thorpe's face, and the expression which appeared there informed him that the rancher had been unaware of his real identity. He smiled when Thorpe uttered an oath, and stood holding the butt of his holstered gun while Thorpe cursed.

The rancher lifted his left arm and pointed his index finger at Manning, who tensed. Then Thorpe crooked his finger and a small hideout gun slid from out of his sleeve and slipped neatly into his hand.

Manning's heart thudded crazily against his ribs as he hurled himself sideways to the left, reaching for his gun even as he moved. He went down on the boards of the porch with a thump. He saw Thorpe's hand following his movement, the squat muzzle of the small .41 calibre weapon in his hand almost sniffing out his direction. He threw up his gun-filled right hand and triggered his Colt, firing three quick shots.

Thorpe's gunhand jerked sideways under the ripping impact of the bullets as they penetrated his chest, and, when his weapon fired, the bullet smacked harmlessly into the front of the house. Thorpe spun and fell into the dust of the yard, his arms outflung, and blood ran from him in a thin stream.

Manning heard the sound of approaching hooves and looked around.

He saw a dozen riders pounding into the yard and pushed himself to his feet, moving quickly to the shelter of the front door of the house. Then he paused, for he recognized Doc Hoyt with the leader, who was wearing a deputy sheriff badge.

Manning relaxed then. This was the posse he had asked to be sent to Slashed T. They must have followed Thorpe all the way from his place. He moved to the rocker on the porch and sat down heavily, suddenly aware that he was exhausted, aware, too, that there was much clearing up to do. But the shooting was over, the gunsmoke dissipating. He holstered his hot gun and eased his mind from the high points of alertness and tension that had gripped him from the moment he arrived in Oaktown.

Now, perhaps, he could take off his law badge, at least for a spell, and try to act like any normal man. He had a ranch to check out and neighbours to meet. He exhaled deeply, ridding his lungs of the last strands of gunsmoke, and turned his face into the fresh breeze blowing across the range. Dead man's range, he thought, but changes were in the wind and he could feel the pull of the future, aware that he had the time now to look forward to it.

THE END

Other titles in the
Linford Western Library:

THE CHISELLER

Tex Larrigan

Soon the paddle-steamer would be on its long journey down the Missouri River to St Louis. Now, all Saul Rhymer had to do was to play the last master-stroke of the evening. He looked at the mounting pile of gold and dollar bills and again at the cards in his hand. Then, looking around the table, he produced the deed to the goldmine in Montana. 'Let's play poker!' But little did he know how that journey back to St Louis would change his life so drastically.

THE ARIZONA KID

Andrew McBride

When former hired gun Calvin Taylor took the job of sheriff of Oxford County, New Mexico, it was for one reason only — to catch, or kill, the notorious Arizona Kid, and pick up the fifteen hundred dollars reward the governor had secretly offered. Taylor found himself on the trail of the infamous gang known as the Regulators, hunting down a man who'd once been his friend. The pursuit became, in every sense, a journey of death.

BULLETS IN BUZZARDS CREEK

Bret Rey

The discovery of a dead saloon girl is only the beginning of Sheriff Jeff Gilpin's problems. Fortunately, his old friend 'Doc' Holliday arrives in Buzzards Creek just as Gilpin is faced by an outlaw gang. In a dramatic shoot-out the sheriff kills their leader and Holliday's reputation scares the hell out of the others. But it isn't long before the outlaws return, when they know Holliday is not around, and C

against six men . . .